PICACHO PEAK MYSTERY

*Kathy,
Keep living the dream.
Joseph A. Mootz
23 Oct 2002*

JOSEPH A. MOOTZ

Living the Dream Publishing

Tucson, Arizona

Copyright © 2003 by Joseph A. Mootz

Published By:

Living the Dream Publishing

PMB 173, 8340 N Thornydale #110

Tucson, Arizona, 85741.

www.livingthedreampublishing.com

ISBN 0-9742080-0-0

Library of Congress Control Number: 2003107268

First Printing

Printed in the United States of America.

Dedication

To my mother who always believed in me more than I believed in myself.

Acknowledgements

Thanks to Gary, John, Julie, Margie, Pat, and Tom for reviewing the first draft of this book and providing constructive criticism about the story and positive encouragement for living the dream.

CHAPTER 1

Josephine Dvorak wiped the sweat from her brow as she waited for her husband Larry to climb over the heavy duty metal gate leading into Picacho Peak State Park. A sign on the gate indicated that the park, located forty miles northwest of Tucson, Arizona, was closed for the summer due to state budget cuts. The closure forced the couple to climb over the locked gate, but also saved them the normal six dollar entry fee.

"Are you sure it's not too hot to do this?" Josephine asked.

"I think we'll be all right," Larry said. He broke into a slow jog to try to catch up to his wife who was walking down the park's paved access road. "Two bottles of water each ought to be enough to keep us hydrated. How hot do you think it'll get?"

"The radio reported it might get into triple digits," Josephine said. "It's ten thirty now and it usually takes us two and a half hours to hike to the top and back, so we should return before the worst of it hits in the late afternoon. I wish we would have started a little earlier this morning."

"Well if you hadn't insisted on cataloging each and every box for the movers to pick up tomorrow, we may have gotten here a little earlier," Larry said.

"Sorry, honey," Josephine said. "You married an engineer remember? Everything has to be in its place before we move on to the next project."

Josephine thought about how they had stayed up late the night before packing their belongings for the move back to their hometown of Cedar Rapids, Iowa. They had a little trouble getting out of bed in the morning after they had stayed up later than usual. When they finally did get up, they scurried around to prepare themselves for a hike to the top of Picacho Peak, their favorite mountain in the Tucson area.

Picacho (pronounced pick-aw-cho), a Spanish word meaning "peak," was the name given to the isolated rock formation northwest of Tucson. They planned the hike as a way to say farewell to the Tucson area before leaving town the next day.

Josephine adjusted the elastic band she used to keep her medium-length dark brown hair in a ponytail behind her head. She pulled on her hair from behind, tightly stretching the lightly freckled skin on her attractive face.

"Besides if your friend Jim, who you know I don't like, had not stopped us as we were pulling out of the driveway we would have saved half an hour," Josephine said.

"At least he gave us those two extra bottles of water," Larry replied. "That saved us from stopping at the store to pick up more."

As they reached the abandoned ranger station a quarter of a mile from the park entrance, they each stopped and took a long drink of water from their separate squeeze bottles. They craned their necks towards the massive saddle-shaped monolith before them and in unison said, "There she is." The eroded lava flow known as Picacho Peak towered more than fifteen hundred feet above them.

Josephine and Larry Dvorak had moved from Iowa to Marana, a suburb of Tucson, when Sungod Industries, an aerospace and defense contractor, offered Josephine a high-paying job as an Electrical

Engineer five years earlier. At the time Josephine had just graduated from the University of Iowa and Larry was working odd jobs as a carpenter. They needed the money and had high hopes that the change in atmosphere would bring new life to their young marriage, which had been strained by financial difficulties and Larry's inconsistent employment.

The move rejuvenated their relationship. Josephine brought home a good salary and received great benefits with plenty of paid time off at Sungod. Larry found work as a carpenter building sets at a local western theme park and installing custom cabinets in houses for the burgeoning housing market in the area. Larry's flexible schedule and Sungod's four ten-hour day workweek allowed the couple to spend three uninterrupted days together every weekend. They spent many of those days hiking the desert trails in the Tucson area.

As they walked through the empty park towards the trailhead, they passed by the empty Recreational Vehicle campground. Josephine thought about the heat again. Normally during the summer they traveled north to the White Mountains near Show Low or the Hualapai Mountains near Flagstaff to hike in a cooler atmosphere. They planned to stop by the White Mountains on the drive back to Cedar Rapids, but they could not resist one last look at the vast Sonoran Desert from top of their favorite peak.

The four small bottles of water they brought with them did not seem to be enough to get them to the top of the peak and back, but Josephine believed her body could survive two and a half hours of sun without failing. She felt fit and trim and had made the hike without struggle at least twice a year for the previous five years. Of course they usually hiked in the fall and spring when the air was cooler. The hot July sun beat down on her bare arms and head as she walked along the black asphalt road.

It was Larry's idea to move back to Iowa after five years in the Tucson area. He received an offer to help build sets for a new amusement park in Cedar Rapids. Similar to the park he worked on in the Tucson area, the small park in Cedar Rapids would celebrate the history of the local area.

Josephine had yet to start seriously looking for new employment. She wanted to take some time off. Although she had not mentioned it to Larry, she recently started feeling a maternal instinct that caused her to wonder if the time was right for them to start a family. Her best friend had taken a year off from Sungod to have a child. Since then Josephine began to notice infants and toddlers everywhere she went. It stirred something inside her. She wanted to wait to see how well Larry could provide for them in the long-term before she brought up the subject.

The couple left the asphalt road at the empty trailhead parking lot and began walking along the dirt trail. The trailhead was marked by a dark brown rectangular sign with white lettering that read,

"HUNTER TRAIL

TO THE TOP OF THE PEAK."

A smaller square sign sporting the same color scheme read,

"HUNTER TRAIL - 2.1 MILES

* STAY ON THE TRAIL * CARRY OUT TRASH

* CARRY ADEQUATE WATER - 2 LITERS RECOMMENDED

* NO HIKING AFTER DARK * NO CAMPING

* TRAVEL AT YOUR OWN RISK

* TRAIL BEYOND SADDLE IS PRIMITIVE

NOT RECOMMENDED FOR CHILDREN UNDER 10, INEXPERIENCED HIKERS, OR DOGS!

CAUTION - DUE TO HEAVY RAINS, PORTIONS
OF THIS TRAIL ARE WASHED OUT. CONTACT
RANGER FOR MORE INFORMATION."

"I think we are each short about a liter of water," Josephine said as she sat down on the rock wall separating the trail from the parking lot. She wiped the sweat from her brow, took a drink of water and stared up at the rocky peak ahead of her.

The mountain looked exactly like a giant horse's saddle. A large saddle-horn-shaped peak pointed to her left as she examined the formation from the north. The sharp peak then gently sloped westward to a curved bottom and then back up to a round ridge. Several smaller triangular shaped peaks trailed off to the west of the saddle-shaped mountain, but Josephine had only one goal in mind. She was determined to reach the saddle-horn-shaped highest point on the peak.

Below the upper ridgeline, sheer cliffs of pink and black stone protected the highest point from any direct assault. The cliffs were a few hundred feet tall themselves and led down to steep slopes covered with vegetation typical of the Sonoran Desert in southern Arizona.

Contrary to popular misconceptions, the desert in southern Arizona is not a barren wasteland. The Sonoran Desert area surrounding the Picacho Peak formation was covered with a rich variety of vegetation. The steep slopes were covered with palo verde trees with olive colored branches and thin needles, chain fruit cholla with long dangerously sharp needles jutting out from all directions on egg-shaped fruit linked together to form branches, prickly pear cacti with flat pancake shaped leaves covered with sharp needles, dark red fishhook barrel cacti with curved flat needles, light green ribbed giant saguaro cacti with closely spaced clusters of three inch long sharp needles, long thin ocotillo with thorny stems spreading in every direction and reaching twenty feet into the sky, and many stemmed creosote bushes with tiny green leaves and small yellow flowers.

Thinking of what lay ahead of her on the trail, Josephine knew that the path she was on led up the steep slopes to the base of the cliffs, circled around under the western ridge of the saddle-shaped peak and then descended a few hundred feet down the south side of the mountain. She knew that on the south side, the trail would take her on a journey to the east up several small steep cliffs to the top of the peak.

"I'll conserve my water so you'll have some if you run out," Larry said wiping his forehead. "Let me have your bottle and I'll pour some of mine into it." He grabbed the quarter full bottle from his wife and poured some of his water into her bottle.

"Don't do me any favors," Josephine said as she took her bottle back. She was a little miffed at the implication that somehow her husband needed to sacrifice himself to take care of her. On the other hand, at least he showed he cared, she thought to herself.

Larry poured a little water on his left hand and then brushed it through his thick black neatly trimmed hair. He set the water bottle on the ground and rubbed his face with both hands. He had not shaved that morning and his square jaw was covered with light stubble. His blue-gray eyes surveyed the area around him as he removed the hands from his face. The bright sun lit up the vast desert within the park boundaries and beyond.

Josephine stood up and walked forward on the trail. She felt irritable and her bladder felt bloated in the hot sun. She tried to focus her mind on her hiking. She wanted to record in her memory the powerful feeling that grew inside her as she hiked the peak.

Larry fell in behind his wife with a smile. He found her very attractive when she was mad at him. He watched her long tan legs as they propelled her up the trail. He felt good about the decision to move back to Iowa. He loved the mild weather of the Tucson area from October through May, but the summer heat in July and August made him irritable.

The trail immediately started up a steep incline through the Sonoran Desert landscape. The tread of the trail consisted of light loose gravel on a cement-hard rock floor. Football-sized sharp jagged rocks lined both sides of the single-lane path. Railroad ties were used as stair-steps along the trail to slow erosion caused by hikers' boots and rain from violent thunderstorms during the monsoon season.

The travelers passed silently by the flowering yellow creosote bushes and dry grass lining the path. The trail tread changed from loose gravel to solid volcanic rock. A chest high steel cable rail appeared along the side of trail to help the hikers maintain their balance as they climbed up steep sharp rocks. A twelve foot tall palo verde tree marked the change in the dynamics of the trail.

Josephine stopped under the shade of the olive green colored limbs of the tree and took another drink of water as she looked to the north back down the path she had traveled. Her husband soon joined her and turned to face the same direction. They stared across the State Park grounds to the Picacho Mountain Range shining in the harsh sunlight a few miles to the north. The triangular shaped mountains stood like pyramids in the desert against a blue sky backdrop. The mountain range stood a few thousand feet above the desert floor at its highest peak and stretched for several miles to the north.

Larry took the lead up the trail. He felt the sweat soak through his light short-sleeved T-shirt and wondered if Josephine was right about the amount of water they brought with them. He could feel the pressure on his feet building as they longed to escape his tight hiking boots.

The two hikers had each left a half-full bottle of water, a dry T-shirt and comfortable footwear in their vehicle for when they returned from the hike. With his shirt already soaked and the pressure building up in his shoes, Larry was anxious to get the hike over with and change into the dry shirt and comfortable sandals.

He was well aware that he and Josephine were not following the recommended guidelines for hiking in the desert. They routinely violated those recommendations in the past and had always gotten away with it. He knew that the experts recommended a hat, long-sleeved shirt, long pants, plenty of sunscreen and a liter of water per hour. He also knew that both he and Josephine were young and healthy and surely would not perish in a few short hours even in the scorching sun.

Larry's lightweight hiking boots scraped over the dark gray lava rock as he made his way up the trail. His right hand lightly grazed along the steel cable rail for balance as his powerful legs propelled him forward. He thought about how nice it would be to feel moisture in the air again back in Iowa. Arizonans liked to brag about their "dry heat" but it took its toll on his skin. He could feel the skin on his arms and face drying and crackling as the hot summer sun beat down on it.

A giant saguaro cactus cast its shadow across the trail and Larry stopped in its shade for a drink. Josephine soon joined him. The pale green giant succulent seemed to take on the form of a massive human being with a thirty inch in diameter trunk over twenty feet tall and giant arms raised in the universal sign of surrender.

The sturdy trunk tempted Larry to stretch out his arm to lean against it for support. The closely spaced clusters of three inch long needles along the saguaro's ribs prevented him from doing so.

Although both the giant saguaro and barrel cacti he saw around him contained reservoirs of water, it was just a fable that the cacti could be easily tapped for their liquid resources. He knew that if their lives depended on it, and he hoped they did not, they would not be able to get water from the desert on this day except for what they had brought with them.

Turning to look back down the trail they had traveled the two hikers could see the outline of the park's asphalt road as it carved a meandering path through the surrounding desert vegetation. The park road was void of traffic due to the park closure. Traffic on the interstate highway just outside of the park, however, zoomed through the hot desert at its usual pace.

Both hikers listened to the sound of automobile traffic passing by. On the opposite side of the interstate, the couple could see the Central Arizona Project canal running parallel to the highway along the foothills of the Picacho Mountain Range. The canal ran from the Colorado River on the western Arizona border to Tucson in southeastern Arizona. It provided water for municipalities and agriculture along its three hundred fifty mile journey.

"How is your water holding out?" Larry asked.

"Well I am three quarters of the way through the first bottle and we have not even reached the saddle yet," Josephine said.

"We will be up in the shade of the cliffs pretty soon," Larry said. "Maybe that will cool things off a little."

Josephine started up the rocky trail without replying. The pink walls of the cliffs faded to light brown as she approached them. She entered a wide but shallow cave at the base of the cliff and sat down on a boulder. She slowly drained the last of the water out of her bottle and handed the empty container to Larry as he approached. Larry swapped the empty bottle for a full one in his fanny pack and handed it to Josephine.

"Nice and cool in here," he said as he took a swig from his still half full bottle.

"Not bad," replied Josephine. "I think we can make it all right if we take it easy. We should be in the shade until we get to the south side and start the big climb."

"Hey, what's that?" Larry said. He pointed towards a parking lot outside the park a few hundred feet down the road from where they had left their silver Sport Utility Vehicle. He reached inside his fanny pack and retrieved his binoculars. "Looks like some kind of water tanker leaving the Indian trading post over there. I thought that place went out of business a few years ago."

"Let me see," Josephine said as she reached for the binoculars. "It's painted all white with no identification. We could sure use some of that water if that's what's inside it." She watched the truck cross under the interstate and then handed the binoculars back to her husband.

"It looked like the kind of tanker truck the developers use to keep the dust down when they are clearing land to put up houses," Larry said. "I think farmers might use them when they are plowing their fields also."

"He was probably called out to provide some water and got lost or was given some bad directions," Josephine said. "There aren't too many housing developments going up in this area, but there is a lot of farmland."

She stood up on her feet, stretched her legs and arms, and then continued her ascent up the trail. Larry fell in behind her.

The two hikers walked east on the relatively flat portion of the trail in the shade along the base of the cliffs. A switchback at the eastern edge of the cliffs reversed the direction of the travelers and increased the incline of the path by a few degrees. The pair reached the saddle of the mountain and sat down on the small wooden bench overlooking the vast expanse of desert to the north and south.

They had completed about half of their journey in elevation and were sitting in the middle of the saddle that separated the rocky peak above them from the lesser peaks below them to the west. They sat for a few minutes without speaking and sipped sparingly from their water bottles.

Josephine stood up and walked to the south side of the saddle towards the ledge overlooking the desert below. From eight hundred feet above the desert floor, she felt like she was looking down from an airplane soon after takeoff. She drew her eyes along the slowly declining ridges to the west that made up the Picacho Peak land formation. The desert floor seemed to turn red, then dirty yellow and then hazy purple as it trailed off to the blue sky horizon dozens of miles in the distance.

It displeased her to think that after climbing over halfway in elevation to the top of the peak, she would now be forced to lose a third of that elevation in climbing down the south side. The peak was formed in such a way that only the most worthy opponent could attain its heights. Josephine became more determined than ever to conquer her monolithic adversary.

She walked to the edge of the trail where the steep downhill incline began, turned to face her husband who was now close behind her, grabbed the steel cable rails on each side of the trail, and then methodically climbed backwards down several hundred feet on the steep rocky path.

The path curved in underneath the cliffs so that beige colored solid rock hung a few feet above Josephine's head. The cliffs provided much needed protection from the sun and Josephine could feel her body temperature diminish and her energy rise as she made her way down the path. The two travelers passed palo verde trees, saguaros and brown grass growing out of solid rock as they made their way to the bottom of the trail.

"Now we begin," Josephine said when she reached the bottom of the steep incline. She swallowed a swig of water from her bottle and walked around the corner of the rocky cliff into the bright sunshine on the south side of the peak.

The hikers traversed the rocky trail eastward over several ridges. The trail was cut into solid gray stone and the travelers proceeded carefully knowing a single misstep would send them sliding down the sharp rocky slope. They passed more giant saguaros spaced at intervals of fifteen to twenty feet along the trail.

Larry looked out across the desert floor to the southwestern horizon. The gray and green irregularly shaped desert floor below him turned to yellow and dark green rectangular farmland. The farm fields faded into a succession of five or more mountain ranges on the horizon.

The closest mountain range included the mountain appropriately named Ragged Top, approximately twenty miles away. Larry knew that behind Ragged Top, which was at least as distinctly shaped and mystical in appearance as Picacho Peak, stood the Silverbell Mountains which reflected a dirty reddish hue in the bright sunlight and was made up of smooth round peaks. The range behind the Silverbells started to fade from red to blue in color with craggy peaks standing much higher on the horizon. A bluish haze obfuscated the succeeding ranges as they faded into the bright blue sky.

Larry knew that the most difficult portion of the trail lay ahead, but he thought that if they could just reach the top and have some water left, the return trip would be easy going. He felt protective of Josephine even though in a lot of ways she was stronger and more capable than he.

He felt that he had let her down by not being as financially successful or ambitious as he should have been in the past. He hoped that the opportunity to get in on the ground floor in the development of the amusement park in Iowa would change all that. If things worked out right, he thought, Josephine could stay home for a few years and they could start a family. He wanted to wait until he really got started on the project before bringing up the subject with her.

Josephine continued in the lead as the couple made their way up a steep incline using the steel cable rail for leverage. She pulled herself up with the cable in her right hand and used her left hand to steady herself on the rough-hewn gray and red rock as she climbed. The cable zigzagged its way up thirty feet in elevation over a forty foot span in distance. Josephine leaned against the yellow colored cliffs at the top and took another drink while she waited for Larry to make the climb.

"Are you doing all right?" Larry asked. Josephine reached out to help pull him up onto the ledge. Both husband and wife breathed heavily from the exertion.

"I'm fine," Josephine replied in between breaths. "Maybe a little light-headed. I might be hyperventilating a little. I did not think the heat would have this much affect on me."

"Let's take a break in the shade up ahead," Larry said as he pointed to a small overhang ahead on the trail. The two moved into the shade and squatted down on their haunches.

"What do you think?" Larry asked. "Are we going to make it?"

Josephine looked at her water bottle which was a little more than a third full. "When this bottle is empty, I think we should turn back," she said. "How much do you have left?"

"I am just emptying, my first bottle," Larry replied as he put the empty bottle in his fanny pack and pulled out the last full bottle. "I think we will be all right if we have half this bottle left when we get to the top. The way back should be easy."

"I've got to pee," Josephine said. "This water is going right through me for some reason." She walked behind a rock formation out of Larry's view.

"Me too," Larry said as he walked a few feet off the trail to relieve himself under a palo verde tree.

A few minutes later, Josephine said, "I am ready. Why don't you take the lead?"

The trail ran along the sharp triangular outcroppings of the cliffs, which were now colored with various shades of red and black. The narrow path led the travelers around a corner such that they faced north and stared at a sheer wall of lava rock forty feet high. A steel cable marked the trail halfway up the wall and then turned towards the right along a ledge and around the corner of the cliff. A length of wire fencing ran along the ledge to protect hikers from falling to their death.

"I'll let you go first on this one," Larry said to Josephine. Josephine grabbed the steel cable with her right hand and began pulling herself up the cliff. Larry followed close behind gently nudging her with his hands.

"Hey, what are you doing down there?" Josephine said.

"Just helping you along," replied Larry. As he reached the ledge he grabbed Josephine's shoulders, turned her face towards him and kissed her passionately on the mouth. After a moment, they both turned to look down the sheer cliff to the desert floor over a thousand feet below.

"I will miss this view," Larry said.

"Is it better than the one you had coming up the cliff?" asked Josephine.

"Not half as good," Larry said and then he kissed her again.

The wire-fence-guarded ledge ran to the eastern corner of the cliff and then turned north again. Josephine climbed over two large jagged boulders into a scene which was now very familiar to her after so many hikes up the peak.

The cliffs below the rocky peak were only a few dozen feet high. They formed a semi-circle with its opening towards the south. Saguaro cacti and young palo verde trees dotted the steep gravelly slopes below the cliffs. The trail followed the base of the cliffs around the western end of the semi-circle to the northern end in the shade. At that point two steel cable rails ran up a twenty five foot sheer cliff to the ledge above. The couple followed the trail around and then sat down on a boulder near the cables.

"I always liked this part of the trail the best," Larry said.

He took a swig of water from the still nearly full bottle and noticed that Josephine's bottle still had some water left. He noted the change in colors of the cliffs from dirty red on the southwestern end to almost purple on the northeastern end.

Josephine pulled herself up the twenty five foot jagged cliff first. Larry soon followed and both stood in the bright sunshine breathing heavily for a moment before proceeding on. The trail followed a steep incline to the north past creosote bushes and fishhook barrel cacti. The travelers crossed another ledge with a wire fence protecting them from a fall of fifty feet or more.

At last the weary hikers reached the middle portion of the saddle-shaped peak. They looked westward towards the butt end of the saddle below them. A single lane dirt path ran from the middle of the saddle to the minor peak to the west. The two hikers then turned their attention to the trail running east to the horn of the saddle. They knew that they were very close to their destination.

"Guess what? I am out of water and I have to pee again," Josephine said. She stepped behind a saguaro for a few minutes and then returned to the trail.

"I still have over two-thirds of mine left," Larry said. "Do you want to press on? We are almost there."

"Let's do it," Josephine said.

The couple struggled up the steep single lane trail over switchbacks that criss-crossed the surface of the peak. Except for the top of the peak ahead of them, nothing for miles around equaled their height above the desert floor.

They could clearly make out the park road and interstate highway as the trail meandered to the northern edge of the precipice. Within a few minutes they reached the pinnacle of the peak.

A large jagged black boulder sat on the northeastern corner of the flat rectangular fifty square foot area at the top. A row of small gray jagged boulders ran down the center of the area. Josephine walked to the east end of the jagged rocks and sank down with her back against the end boulder.

"Are you all right?" Larry asked. He pushed his half empty bottle to her lips.

After a swallow of water, Josephine wiped the sweat from her brow and shook her head in the affirmative.

Larry looked at his watch. It was one o'clock in the afternoon. It had taken them over two and a half hours to climb the peak in the hot sun. On a cooler day it would take half that long. Larry stood up and took in the scenery around him for the last time.

Large square farm fields spread out fifteen hundred feet below him from the northeast to the southeast around the interstate exit that led to the small town known as Red Rock. The fields were alternately colored dark brown, golden, and dark green depending on whether they were freshly plowed, had wheat ready to harvest, or were covered with healthy cotton plants. On the eastern horizon Larry could see the Tortolita Mountains near his home in Marana. Past the Tortolita's, the massive Santa Catalina Mountains stood as guardians over the city of Tucson and the surrounding area. The Tucson Mountains on the western edge of the city were also visible from the peak.

Larry turned his gaze towards the direction of the Picacho Mountain Range across the interstate to the north. A white speck on the desert floor between the interstate and the mountain range caught his eye. He retrieved his binoculars from his fanny pack and zoomed in on the speck.

A white unmarked water tanker came into focus. It looked like the tanker they had earlier observed leaving the Indian trading post and crossing under the interstate near the park entrance. A green hose ran from the back end of the truck over a chain-link fence and into the Central Arizona Project canal.

Larry scanned his binoculars towards the front of the truck and saw a man wearing a green camouflage outfit staring back at him with his own set of binoculars. Larry jerked the binoculars away from his eyes and then slowly brought them back into focus. He scanned the area around the truck and saw a similarly dressed man with a rifle slung over his shoulder.

A nauseous feeling suddenly grew in the pit of his stomach. He bent over and vomited small amount of sticky liquid onto the ground. He stood up straight and regained his composure.

"Let's get out of here," he said as he turned back towards Josephine.

Josephine was laying on her back on the jagged rocks. At her husband's command she struggled to sit up straight. Larry gently lifted his wife to a sitting position and held the nearly empty bottle of water to her lips.

CHAPTER 2

Johnny Blue drove his red pickup truck along Frontage Road on the north side of Intertsate-10. He was driving directly towards the oddly-shaped mountain known as Picacho Peak. From his viewpoint, the peak looked like a giant sore thumb sticking out of the surrounding flat desert. The highest point on the eastern edge of the land formation curved like a broken thumbnail out over the cliffs that guarded it from below.

As Johnny drove along the quiet two-lane road towards the mountain, the peak's shape changed to that of a cupped hand, then to the shape of the top half of a giant egg, and finally to the shape, so familiar to passersby on the interstate, of a horse's saddle. He tried to keep one eye on the road and one on the peak as he drove so as to not miss the transformation of the mountain into its many shapes.

Picacho Peak's odd shape and isolation in the surrounding desert had long made it a welcome navigation point for desert travelers including ancient Native Americans and early Spanish Missionaries. Johnny tried to imagine all the activities that must have transacted around the peak over the years. He thought about Native Americans hunting game and carving art into the cliffs and boulders in the surrounding area. He thought about the Spanish Missionaries making camp for the night on their way to California in the early eighteen hundreds. He thought of the Civil War battle in which thirteen Confederate soldiers from Tucson repelled ten Union soldiers from California in a two hour long skirmish near the peak.

His thoughts turned to the millions of automobile drivers that whizzed by the peak every year on the interstate between Tucson and Phoenix. The peak dominated the view from the freeway as travelers drove by or stopped at the small gift shops at the freeway exit to the State Park that surrounded the peak.

Johnny parked his pickup in front of the locked heavy duty metal gate at the entrance to the State Park at exactly four o'clock on a hot Sunday afternoon in July. The magnetic sign on the side of his pickup and the blue patch on the arm of his neatly pressed white shirt identified him as an employee of the Faithful Security Agency based in Marana, Arizona. His graying temples and slightly wrinkled but handsome face identified him as a man who had lived a hard life.

He had completed half of his regular patrol route which included checking the security of the Central Arizona Project canal and Picacho Peak State Park. The stop at the park was added to his route after the park was closed for the summer due to state budget cuts. He patrolled the same route once a night on Friday evenings and three times a day on Saturdays and Sundays.

Johnny verified the status of the padlock holding the two heavy arms of the gate together and then surveyed the surrounding area. A silver SUV parked along the road outside of the State Park caught Johnny's attention. The vehicle was parked in front of the closed gate leading to the parking lot of a tourist gift shop that was closed for the season. Johnny backed up his pickup and parked it next to the SUV. He picked up his handheld radio and called into the dispatcher.

"There is a silver Toyota FourRunner parked suspiciously in front of the gift shop outside the State Park," Johnny spoke into the heavy black radio. "I am going to check it out."

"What's so suspicious about the way they parked it, detective," the dispatcher responded through the radio. "Did they park on the white line?"

Johnny had grown accustomed to the good natured ribbing he received from Charlie Jones, the weekend dispatcher. He knew that Charlie thought that Johnny took his part-time job a little too seriously. He had made his opinion very clear ever since Johnny started the job two months earlier.

The job was more than a part-time gig to Johnny. Since the September 11, 2001 terrorist attacks, he felt an obligation to do his part to protect the country from future attacks. He made sure that he reported even the slightest bit of suspicious activity on his patrol of the State Park and the Central Arizona Project canal. His hope was that he could contribute to the overall security of the country as one of the many eyes and ears reporting to higher authorities. He also hoped that those higher authorities were communicating among themselves to help prevent any repeat attacks.

The Central Arizona Project canal is managed by the federal government's Bureau of Reclamation. The Bureau is responsible for managing water related resources including dams, hydroelectric power plants and canals throughout the western United States. After the September 11, 2001 attacks, the security of the resources managed by the Bureau of Reclamation became of interest to the newly formed Homeland Security Department. The department had analyzed the security of the resources and suggested improvements, one of which resulted in the creation of Johnny's part-time job as a security guard for the CAP canal.

"Well for one thing the gift shop is closed for the season and it is a hundred and seven degrees out here," Johnny said. "There is no reason for anybody to be out in this heat."

"All right, check it out but don't do anything stupid," Charlie responded. "I don't want you getting mixed up with any illegal alien smugglers or vigilantes. Just make sure there are no dead bodies in the vehicle and that the park gate is secure and then continue on your rounds."

Johnny Blue stepped out of his red pickup and into the blazing afternoon sun. He grabbed his plastic squeeze bottle of water, donned his wide brimmed hat for protection from the sun, rolled down the sleeves of his shirt, and situated his mirrored sunglasses on his nose. Charlie's reminder about the trouble with illegal alien smugglers from Mexico and American militia groups acting as vigilantes caused Johnny to survey the surrounding area closely.

Recently several illegal aliens were killed by unknown persons near the small town of Red Rock only five miles away from Picacho Peak. The report of the incident put Johnny and other people living in remote areas on alert.

Red Rock really was not a town at all. It was formed in the early twentieth century so that the local farmers would have a place to pick up their mail. The only other service the town provided was a small bar near the interstate. The irregular hours and unkempt appearance of the drinking establishment kept all but the most desperate local residents away. Any other services the locals needed required them to drive twenty miles farther down the interstate to the town of Marana.

Johnny knew that the incident at Red Rock involved illegal aliens being attacked as they waited for smugglers to pick them up for transfer after they traveled from Mexico into the United States. By the time they reached the area around Red Rock, the illegal border crossers would have traveled nearly a hundred miles across the barren desert on foot. The area around

Red Rock was notorious as a place for smugglers to pick up their cargo and transport them up the interstate to the Phoenix area for distribution across the United States.

According to newspaper reports, police had few leads on the case. A lot of local residents thought that either greedy smugglers had killed their charges for their money or vigilante groups had taken the law into their own hands to try to stem the tide of illegal immigration. Johnny Blue wanted no part of either suspected group.

As he stepped out of his truck, Johnny noticed a two-foot long trail of small blue crystals running along the asphalt road parallel to the SUV about two feet to the left of the vehicle. He looked closely at the crystals, but did not recognize them as anything he had seen before. They looked a little to large to be laundry detergent, but he was not sure.

Johnny walked around the vehicle and shaded his eyes with his hand as he tried to peer through the vehicle's tinted windows. All he received for his efforts was a view of the reflection of his mirrored sunglasses. He pushed the glasses back on his nose and walked towards the front of the vehicle.

"Hello! Anyone around," he yelled. No one answered his call.

Looking through the front windshield into the vehicle Johnny noticed two half full bottles of water resting in the cup holders in the console between the driver's seat and passenger seat. A ladies T-shirt and sandals lay on the passenger seat. Johnny stood on his toes to look through the steering wheel to the drivers' side of the vehicle. A man's T-shirt and sandals lay on the driver's seat.

"Hey Charlie, looks like we have a couple hikers trespassing in the State Park," Johnny said into his radio.

"What do you want me to do, call the cops?" Charlie said.

"You know they won't come out on a simple trespass charge," Johnny replied. "It's a hundred and seven degrees out here. Based on the clothes they left in their car, it looks like a man and a woman. They could be in trouble if they didn't bring at least a couple of gallons of water with them."

"That's the second time you've mentioned the exact temperature. Do you have a new secret decoder ring with a thermometer you are trying to show off?" Charlie said. "Let me report the trespass to the sheriff and you continue on your rounds."

"I'm going to go in and take a look around the park," Johnny said as he returned to his pickup.

"What are you going to do, hike up to the top of the peak yourself to make sure they have enough water?" Charlie said through the radio. "I am already reporting this to the sheriff so continue on your rounds. Do you read me?"

"You are breaking up Charlie," Johnny said. "That last transmission was garbled. I think maybe sunspots are affecting my reception. I'll call you back in fifteen minutes after they have subsided."

"You listen to me Johnny. You get back out on your rounds immediately or your part-time ass is fired," Charlie's voice came out of the radio speaker.

Johnny switched the receiver off and sat down behind the steering wheel of his pickup truck. He drove forward to the State Park gate and got back out of the vehicle. He unlocked the padlock holding the two arms of the gate together and then got back in his pickup and drove slowly into the park.

With his bare eyes Johnny scanned the ditch along the road as he drove towards the ranger station. No sign of human life came from the dry grass in the ditch along the road. He turned left past the station and drove towards the Hunter Trailhead. A few minutes later he parked his vehicle in the trailhead parking lot.

Johnny grabbed his binoculars from the dashboard in front of him and stepped out of the pickup. He raised the binoculars to his eyes and then systematically explored the trail a foot at a time. He only moved his gaze fifty feet up the trail before he saw what looked like two hiking boots with their toes pointed towards the sky. Johnny returned the binoculars to the dashboard of his pickup and walked cautiously towards the boots.

As he closed in on the footwear, he saw a man in his late twenties, wearing shorts and a T-shirt, sitting straight up with his back against a large boulder. The hot afternoon sun beat down on the man's red face. Johnny turned his radio back on.

"Charlie I've found the body of a dead man out here," Johnny said into the radio as he felt for a pulse on the dead man's neck. "Get a search and rescue unit and the sheriff out here right away. There may be a woman in trouble in the area also."

CHAPTER 3

After discovering the dead man's body, Johnny started up the trail towards the peak under the assumption that the woman may have collapsed before the man and could still be alive. He found what looked and smelled like human vomit a few hundred feet up the path. When he turned around to survey his progress on the trail, he saw the woman's body sitting upright in the ravine between the Hunter Trailhead and the Calloway Trail a few yards to the east. The woman had outlasted her companion by fifty feet.

Johnny walked back down the trail and crossed the ravine to verify that the woman had expired. From the marks on the ground near the body, he imagined that she had panicked when the man collapsed and then tried to cut across the ravine as a shortcut to the SUV. She must have stumbled to the ground and then brought herself up to a sitting position to recover. She expired before she ever got going again.

He recognized the woman as Josephine Dvorak, a former co-worker from Sungod Industries. Her face was red and her lips parched as she sat in the upright position on the desert floor. Johnny had met the woman briefly a few years earlier when he worked at the aerospace and defense contractor before his early retirement. He did not know much about her except that she worked in the same department as he and attended the same department meetings. He assumed her male companion was her husband who he had never met, but he would let the sheriff verify his identity.

Johnny called in the discovery of the second body but told the dispatcher not to call off the search and rescue team since there was a chance someone else accompanied the two on their death march. Johnny did not like to take chances. Sometimes people told him he worried too much, but he always lived by the axiom that it was better to be safe than sorry.

He examined the body closely to see if there were any signs of injuries that may have caused her to sit down and die in the heat of the afternoon. He noticed a half a dozen spots of dried blood on her calf just below the bottom of her shorts. Any one of a dozen or more desert plants could have caused the minor damage with their sharp needles. He saw no other signs of injury to the dead woman.

Johnny returned to the dead man and examined him for injury. He noticed a few spots of dried blood on the tips of the man's fingers. The pinprick-like marks looked similar to the marks on the woman's leg. Using his best deductive reasoning techniques, Johnny decided that the fruit of a "jumping cholla" must have attached itself to the woman's leg and the man must have injured his fingers helping her dislodge it.

The "jumping cholla" was another name for the chain fruit cholla, a plant whose fruit looked like a small hand grenade covered with three-inch long needle-like spikes. The fruit had a reputation of jumping out at passersby and digging its spikes into the soft flesh of legs or arms. The spikes were difficult to remove because they would dig into the flesh in every conceivable direction. Pulling out one spike would cause the other spikes to dig deeper into the flesh.

He looked the dead man over and realized his attire provided little protection from the sun. He would probably be okay with the shorts, but the absence of any head or arm protection disturbed Johnny. He looked back towards the dead woman and realized she was similarly attired.

Johnny was a big believer in keeping himself hydrated in the dry desert air. As hot as it was and by the way they were dressed, Johnny thought they would have needed a large amount of water to survive any amount of time out in the afternoon sun. He looked around the area and saw no signs of bottles with which to carry water. Using his deductive reasoning again he assumed the couple could have run out of water farther up the trail and discarded the empty bottles in the desert. The man had on a fanny pack that could hold a few bottles, but not near enough to hike the peak on such a hot day.

Johnny left the dead man and sat down on the wooden bench of a picnic table in the shade of the Saguaro Ramada near the start of the trail. Each picnic area in the park contained its own concrete ramada named after a Sonoran Desert plant. The ramada was open at two ends with walls and a roof made out of concrete and painted the same beige color as the restrooms on the other side of the park. The air felt twenty degrees cooler in the shade of the structure.

The only dead people Johnny had seen in his life were those of his wife and child at their funeral three years earlier. Seeing his former co-worker lying in the hot sun brought back memories of the accident that took the lives of his family members.

Josephine's facial structure was similar to his wife Carol's. A blurry vision of Josephine's face juxtaposed with Carol's face flashed through his mind. He tried to push the vision away with pleasant thoughts of his life with Carol. He sipped water from his squeeze bottle and tried to think of the times he and Carol had climbed Picacho Peak together before their son Jerry came along.

Carol was young and pretty when Johnny met her in college in Oregon. She had long flowing silky red hair and a thin attractive face with soft skin. They married just after graduation. They moved to Marana soon after college when Johnny got a job as a Software Engineer with Sungod Industries.

During their first few years in the Tucson area they spent a lot of weekends hiking in the desert. Picacho Peak was one of their favorite hikes due to the variety of the terrain, the spectacular views and difficulty of the trail. When their son Jerry came along a few years later, they slowed down on the hiking for a while. Their son had just turned five years old and they were thinking about taking him with them on a hike to the top of the peak when the accident took the lives of the boy and Carol.

Johnny's thoughts were interrupted by a sheriff's car pulling into the parking lot next to his pickup. Johnny greeted Deputy Sheriff Juan Dugas as the officer stepped out of the car onto the black asphalt in the Hunter Trailhead parking lot. The tall and slim deputy with a bronze complexion surveyed the area with his dark eyes as he stepped out of his patrol car.

Johnny remembered passing by the sheriff's car on Park Link Drive as he left the Red Rock Pumping Plant on the Central Arizona Project canal earlier on his patrol. He thought nothing of it at the time but now he was glad that the deputy was in the area and able to respond quickly to his call.

He led the deputy to the two bodies and told him how he found them. He told the deputy about the vomit he found on the trail, the wounds on the woman's leg and the man's hand, and the clothes in the front seat of the vehicle outside the park. He also mentioned his insecurity about whether there were other hikers to look for.

"We'll let search and rescue handle that," the deputy said. "When I first got the call about dead bodies in the desert, I thought it might be another incident of illegal aliens attacking each other or maybe one of them dying of thirst in the desert again. I spend more time responding to complaints from people that don't belong here than from people that do belong here.

"I hate to see something like this though. These look like good people."

"Why don't you fill this out over there in the shade and let us look into this," the deputy said as he handed Johnny a witness form to fill out. "You look a little upset. Are you going to be all right?"

"I'll be all right," Johnny said. He walked slowly back to the ramada. He wanted to get out of the heat and erase the vision of Josephine's scarlet red face juxtaposed with the face of his wife Carol.

He sat down at the picnic table and began to fill out the form. As he wrote down the details of his discovery, he thought about what the sheriff said about illegal aliens. In the last few months he had heard several reports of deaths of illegal aliens, or "undocumented immigrants" as the politically correct press liked to refer to them. Johnny wondered if someday political correctness would progress to the point where the illegal aliens would simply be referred to as "immigrants" and then later "citizens."

According to the news reports, many of the deaths were the result of the illegals crossing the desert at the wrong time of year with inadequate water. This occurred even after a charitable organization had been formed to put stations of water at pivotal points in the desert in an effort to prevent the deaths.

Johnny thought that the efforts of the group were misguided, if not criminal. It was like those lab experiments with rats, if you rewarded them with enough sugar water eventually the rats would shock themselves to death to get at it. Putting a few gallons of water in the desert just encouraged the illegals to abandon their situation in Mexico to become part of the American dream at any cost. The water would never be enough to save the hundreds of thousands of immigrants that crossed the desert in Arizona every year.

Johnny had sincere compassion for the illegals. They were caught between a government that could not manage its own economy in a way that allowed its citizens to provide for their families and the tempting prize of good pay for hard work by crossing the border to the north. From the stories Johnny had read, crossing the border was a difficult and expensive endeavor.

The border crossers were required to pay exorbitant fees for smugglers to lead them across dozens of miles of harsh desert to pick-up spots along the interstate between Tucson and Phoenix. From there they would be forced to pay another smuggler, known as a *coyote*, to transfer them along the interstate to Phoenix for distribution to farms and sweatshops around the country to earn money for their families back in Mexico. Over the last few weeks Johnny had heard of at least two incidents of *coyotes* wrecking their dangerously overloaded vehicles on the interstate killing or severely injuring dozens of their passengers.

To add to the plight of the border crossers, farmers and other landowners were now encouraging members of militia groups to patrol their land to try to scare the illegals back over the border. Johnny had seen news reports of the militia members wearing camouflage hunting outfits and holding high-powered rifles patrolling the desert area near the border. The State Police and Border Patrol had made it clear that the militia and other American citizens had no legal standing to detain anyone, including those in the country illegally, and that they were required to obey all laws regarding trespassing on state or private land.

There had been no reports of the vigilantes ever accosting any illegals, but one group of militia men did force a small group of drug smugglers to abandon the bales of marijuana they were smuggling across a cattle ranch. They reported the incident to the State Police and turned the contraband over to them.

Most of the militia groups were stationing themselves on ranches close to the border. Johnny did not think any of the groups would be operating as far north as the Red Rock and Picacho Peak area.

A recent incident near the agricultural community of Red Rock had heightened the anxiety of border crossers. A group of two dozen or more border crossers were attacked while they hid in the desert near the interstate waiting to be picked up by a *coyote*. Two of the border crossers were killed while one escaped to tell the American authorities. The rest of the border crossers simply disappeared.

Red Rock was only a few miles east of Picacho Peak. Johnny hoped that the killing of the illegals was an isolated incident. He hoped that the sheriff or whoever was responsible for investigating the crime would solve it soon. He wondered who was involved in investigating the crime. Was it the Border Patrol or the State Police? Surely the Pinal County Sheriff's Department did not have enough manpower to do an adequate job.

Picacho Peak and Red Rock are located in sparsely populated Pinal County. The peak is only forty miles from the densely populated Tucson metropolitan area in Pima County and sixty five miles from the even more densely populated Phoenix area in Maricopa County. Located on the southwestern edge of Pinal County, the economy of the area around Picacho Peak and Red Rock is primarily based on agriculture. Cattle ranches and cotton fields provide the major source of income for local residents.

The Pinal County Sheriff's Office reflects the second class status of the largely rural county. The resources of the small sheriff's office are hard pressed to cover the thousands of square miles of area they are charged with protecting. The department relies heavily on the crime investigation services of the Arizona Department of Public Safety, commonly known as the State Police.

Johnny knew that since September 11, 2001, the Homeland Security Department promised to open the lines of communication between law enforcement agencies investigating separate but possibly related incidents pertaining to national security. As part of his security guard training he was instructed to report all incidents no matter how trivial. He was told that all information would be passed along to the Homeland Security Department in hopes that someone looking at the big picture could piece together enough information to prevent future attacks on the country. He wondered if anyone was looking at the big picture in relation to the illegal alien killings.

Johnny stood up and stretched his arms above his head after filling out the form the deputy gave him. He made sure that he included every detail he could remember when he filled out the form in case there was something more sinister going on than just a simple case of death by dehydration in the desert. He included the information about finding the blue crystals near the SUV.

"I've got to finish my rounds," he said as he handed the report to Deputy Dugas. "I put in what I saw in the FourRunner. I also noticed some crystals on the pavement next to the vehicle. It's probably nothing, but I wanted you to know in case you want to check it out."

"It looks like a pretty clear case of heat stroke," the deputy replied. "The red dry skin on the victims and the vomit you found further up the trail are symptoms I've seen too many times before. Those kids were crazy to be out in this heat with bare arms and heads. I found four empty bottles of water in their pack. A couple of more might have helped them last long enough to make it back to their vehicle."

"What about the way they were propped up like that?" Johnny asked. "It's almost as if they just sat down and died."

"That's not uncommon," the deputy replied. "People become pretty delusional when heat exhaustion starts to set in. Sometimes they'll sit down thinking they just need to rest for a few minutes and then they never get up again."

"Did you notice the spots of blood on the woman's leg and the man's fingers?" Johnny asked.

"Yes I did," the sheriff replied. "They probably got caught by a cholla or something."

"That's what I thought," Johnny said.

As Johnny turned to walk back to his pickup, a white Arizona Department of Public Safety Ford Crown Victoria vehicle pulled into the parking lot next to the sheriff's vehicle. Johnny recognized Officer Mike Gerrity as he stepped out of the automobile. Gerrity's tall heavyset frame with broad shoulders strode confidently towards the deputy sheriff. His light skinned face had a pinkish hue as his green eyes surveyed the surrounding area.

Johnny remembered meeting the officer at the scene of the tragic car crash that killed his wife and young son three years earlier. He remembered driving out to the scene of the multi-car accident caused by a violent dust storm on the interstate between Tucson and Phoenix. He thought back to how the officer put his arm around his shoulder as he sobbed uncontrollably in grief over his loss. He also remembered the officer's calls to his house to make sure he was all right in the weeks after the incident.

Johnny waved hello to the State Police Officer as Gerrity walked towards Deputy Dugas. The officer waved back and smiled. Johnny wondered if he remembered where they had met.

CHAPTER 4

Johnny Blue drove his red pickup truck out of Picacho Peak State Park. He drove under the interstate to the road on the north side of the freeway. He stopped at the stop sign and then turned left away from the combination restaurant, gas station and tourist gift shop at the intersection. He drove slowly down the two-lane asphalt road running parallel to the freeway. Normally by this time in the evening he would have finished his rounds and stopped by the restaurant to eat his evening meal and to flirt and gossip with Marcie, the owner of the establishment. Tonight he did not feel like eating, flirting or gossiping.

Johnny thought about how he came to be the weekend security patrol for the Central Arizona Project canal. The previous year he took an early retirement from Sungod Industries, sold his house in Marana, and bought ten acres of secluded desert land on Park Link Drive. He was fifty five years old and had worked for Sungod for ten years. The money from his early retirement and from the settlement on the accident that killed his wife and son would let him live his life without the day-to-day worry of a steady income.

He had enough money to live without working, but when he saw the advertisement in the paper for the part-time job near his home he felt it would be a good distraction from the activities of writing short stories and building a straw-bale house on his new property. He liked solitude, peace and quiet, but he knew himself well enough to know that he occasionally needed human interaction to remain sane.

Johnny wiped the sweat from his brow and turned off of the asphalt road onto a dirt road that led to the Picacho Mountain Range and the Central Arizona Project canal. He opened the white aluminum tubing gate, drove through the opening in the fence, and then locked the gate behind him. The gate led to a dirt road on private land managed by the State of Arizona as State Trust Land. The land was used by a cattle rancher to raise range cattle but hunters, campers, and CAP employees were allowed access to the land for their specific uses.

He drove slowly down the rough road. His pickup truck shook violently from the washboard-like surface of the hard rocky road. He tried to keep visions of Josephine Dvorak's parched face out of his head. He remembered that the few times he saw her at Sungod she had a great smile and a body that was nice to look at. Somehow their paths had never crossed at the giant aerospace company until after his wife Carol died. He never noticed the similarity in the faces of the two women until he found Josephine dead on the trail in the State Park. A vision of the faces of the two women flashed through his mind again.

Johnny remembered that Josephine had a reputation as a solid engineer that produced above average work. He could not understand how someone so young and fit could die of heat exhaustion in such a short time, even in the summer heat of southern Arizona. He also could not understand how someone so intelligent and logical could be out in the desert without proper attire or adequate water.

He drove across a deep sandy wash making sure to keep his acceleration at an even level so as not to get stuck or kick up too much dust. It always irritated him to see hunters or farmers driving down sandy dirt roads at sixty miles an hour as if they would get stuck in the sand if they even hinted at easing up on the accelerator. That kind of driving kicked up more dust in the atmosphere. Although the air quality in the area was considered good, the clear cutting and reshaping of the land by developers and the plowing by farmers kicked up enough particulates in the air to make visibility on the roads and breathing the dusty air hazardous to one's health.

After two miles of driving along the dirt road, Johnny stopped his pickup at the locked gate leading to the canal access road. He unlocked the padlock and chain holding the chain link gate closed, swung open the gate and drove through the opening in the fence to the canal access road. He closed and locked the gate behind him and then returned to his pickup.

"Picacho Patrol reporting Checkpoint Delta all secure," Johnny said into the radio. He had already reported the status of Checkpoints Alpha though Charlie earlier on his tour. Checkpoint Charlie was the gate at the State Park and Alpha and Bravo were the gates to the canal access road near the Red Rock Pumping Plant off of Park Link Drive. He had visited the latter two checkpoints earlier on his patrol on his way to the State Park.

His duties on the patrol included checking the canal's locks, gates, fences and lining for signs of damage. He also looked for any suspicious activity by trespassers and for debris floating in the canal. The canal was eighty feet wide at the top, twenty four feet wide at the bottom, and the water was sixteen feet deep. His patrol area covered the canal as it ran from the Brady Pumping Plant ten miles away on the northwest side to the Picacho Pumping Plant in the foothills of the Picacho Mountain Range and down to the Red Rock Pumping Plant a few miles past Park Link Drive on the southeast end.

The three pumping plants formed a trio of facilities used to supply water to the farmers in southeastern Pinal County and to pass water along to the Tucson metropolitan area and farmers in Pima County. Water only flowed in the canal when the pumping plants along its three hundred fifty mile length pumped it from one section to the next. When the pumping plants were not in operation, the water in the canal sat stagnant waiting for delivery.

The pumping plants were synchronized by a master control center in Phoenix. Farmers were required to order water for their crops at least a week in advance. The request would be programmed into the system and at the appropriate time the proper gates would automatically be opened and water pumped from the canal to the farmer's irrigation ditches.

The Central Arizona Project canal started out as a plan for Arizona to keep from losing its claim on allotted water from the Colorado River. The project had its share of controversy since its proposal in the late nineteen sixties. The canal was completed in the late nineteen eighties, but at the time the farmers could get water cheaper by continuing to pump it from the ground. They also had a natural tendency to shy away from letting the government control their water supply. On the other hand, residents of the large municipalities in the area shied away from using the water due to fear of contamination of their water supply.

As the water table began to fall sharply in the early nineteen nineties farmers and the City of Tucson began to purchase CAP water. It took the City of Tucson two trial periods over a period of ten years and surviving a local law that angry citizens had passed against the use of CAP water before the city began to use the water on a regular basis. The law was passed in the aftermath of the first trial period in which the plumbing in several Tucson neighborhoods was ruined. The cause of the problem was later discovered to be the reverse flow of water in Tucson's water pipes tearing off calcified debris and sending it into the plumbing of the local houses.

A long drought and pressure from developers to sell their land for housing developments motivated the farmers to begin using the CAP water. Many farmers, however, gave into the lure of quick profits and sold out to developers instead. Urban sprawl took over the Tucson area and its surrounding suburbs in the early nineteen nineties. The primarily agricultural town of Marana, only twenty miles southeast of Picacho Peak, was named the fastest growing city in Arizona in the nineteen nineties after its population quadrupled to over ten thousand residents.

In the winter months the population of greater Tucson swelled by twenty five percent as "snowbirds" flocked to its mild winter climate. Snowbirds, residents of northern states who wintered in the area, demanded permanent housing and had the money to purchase it. Developers scrambled to buy cotton farms, national and state land reserves, and any land they could get their hands on to meet the demands of their wealthy clients from the north.

Much of the farmland in Marana had been purchased by developers in recent years. Johnny remembered reading a newspaper editorial a few months earlier that described how developers that purchased agricultural land inherited the tax exemptions associated with such land.

The editorial told the story of the case of a parcel of land south of Tucson bought by Red Ruby Real Estate, one of Arizona's largest land developers. The developer bought two thousand acres and submitted a plan to build four thousand houses. Red Ruby received millions of dollars by trading or selling hundreds of acres of land to the federal government. Most of the land the developer dumped came from the least-valuable portion of the proposed development. The total tax bill the developer paid while making millions of dollars was less than a dollar an acre and he had yet to build a house.

Johnny wondered if the next logical expansion area could be the cotton fields and cattle ranches surrounding Red Rock or the desert wilderness along Park Link Drive. If he had a choice, he hoped it would be the former not the latter. He would prefer no developments in either area since that would only encourage more activity near the desert ranch on which he was trying to live a life of peace and solitude.

"How are you holding up out there?" Charlie asked through the radio speaker as Johnny drove northwest along the canal towards the Picacho Pumping Plant.

"I'm doing fine," Johnny replied. "I'll be glad when this shift is over though."

"You've had a hard day. Why don't you take tomorrow off?" Charlie said.

"Thanks a lot wise guy. You know I get the next four days off," Johnny said.

He continued driving northwest along the canal. As he drove he looked for breaks in the perimeter fence, dead animals and signs of suspicious activity.

The summer sun shone down from its position twenty degrees above the western horizon. Everything seemed to be in order on the route to the pumping plants. In the two months he had driven the route nothing much was ever out of order. Once he found a dead coyote caught on one of the barbed wire strands strung across the canal to catch just such debris. The skinny fellow must have slipped down the steep interior bank of the canal into the water and never found enough grip on the angled side walls to climb out.

Johnny remembered using the telescopic pole and rubber gloves in the back of his pickup to retrieve the animal and encase it in a body bag for animal control to pick up the next day. The animal could not have been dead for more than twelve hours, but the stench still made Johnny frown as he remembered it a month later.

"Dispatch, this is Picacho Patrol. Checkpoint Echo all secure," Johnny said into the radio after he made sure all the doors and gates around the Picacho Pumping Plant were secure. He received acknowledgement from the dispatcher and continued on his route.

Johnny drove at the leisurely pace of ten miles per hour to reduce his chance of missing anything. The patrol took around three hours to complete which enabled him to perform it twice a day on his eight hour shift. He reached the Brady Pumping plant, made certain nothing was out of order, and reported Checkpoint Foxtrot all secure. He turned his pickup around and headed back the way he came.

He wondered about the blue crystals he had found in the parking lot near the Dvorak's vehicle. He had not noticed them on his morning patrol and so assumed they must have come from the Dvoraks when they got out of their car. Maybe they had some laundry in the back and some detergent spilled out on the ground when they were changing into their hiking boots, he thought.

Johnny brought his vehicle to a stop at Checkpoint Golf, a gate in the middle of the desert. The gate led to small hill of lava rock known as Wymola Bluff. The bluff was located in the middle of a flat desert valley about halfway between the canal and the interstate highway.

Johnny got out of his pickup and walked over to the gate to check that the padlock was still locked. He pressed the talk button on his radio to report all clear and then stopped himself. A quarter inch wide two foot long trail of blue crystals ran along the sandy surface of the road on the other side of the gate. Johnny unlocked the gate and squatted down to get a closer look at the crystals. They looked like ordinary clothes detergent.

"This is Picacho Patrol. I've found some more of those blue crystals here at Checkpoint Golf," Johnny said into the radio. "I wonder if the sheriff wants to take a look at them."

"What are you trying to do to me," Charlie's voice came through the radio. "All I wanted was a nice relaxing Sunday at my desk and you have to play Sherlock Holmes out there."

"Hey, the book says to report all suspicious activity to the sheriff. Blue crystals along a canal in the middle of the desert where no one should be are suspicious," Johnny said. "So get the sheriff on the phone and find out what he wants to do about it."

"Hang on a minute," Charlie said.

Johnny surveyed the area while he waited for Charlie's response. Deep tire tracks in the sand led away from the gate towards the three hundred foot tall Wymola Bluff. By the lack of debris on the tracks, Johnny knew that they could not be more than a day old. The tracks appeared to be made by a truck with four wheels on its rear axle.

"The sheriff already left Picacho Peak to investigate another shooting of illegals near Red Rock," Charlie's voice came through the radio speaker. "He wants to know if you can take some pictures of the scene and gather up a sample of the crystals for him and he'll have someone check it out tomorrow."

"All right. Tell him to have someone swing by my place on Park Link Drive tomorrow morning to pick this stuff up," Johnny said.

"That's right. You've got the big ranch out in the middle of the desert don't you?" Charlie responded.

"Beats living in some ticky-tacky subdivision full of ticky-tacky houses next to some ticky-tacky smart ass like you," Johnny said. "Tell the sheriff there are some heavy truck tracks leading away from the scene

towards Wymola Bluff. I'd go check it out, but I don't
want to destroy any evidence."

"All right, Sherlock. Why don't you finish your
rounds and go home and get a good night's sleep,"
Charlie said.

Johnny took a half dozen Polaroid shots with the
company provided camera. Then he took several more
shots with his own personal digital camera and marked
a waypoint on his personal Global Positioning System
unit. He collected a small plastic bag full of crystals for
the sheriff and then collected another bag for himself.

He had carried the digital camera in his pickup to
take pictures of sunsets, wildlife and mountains while
on patrol. The GPS unit was a part time hobby he
experimented around with. He had recorded his tracks
on every trail he hiked in the previous five years since
he bought the unit. One of those trails included the
Hunter Trail on Picacho Peak. The same one Josephine
and her husband died on a few hours earlier.

Johnny stared at the peak as the setting sun
threw long shadows around its every curve, crevice and
crag. The peak always held a mystical place in his
heart. As he drove along the canal towards the
southeast, he remembered the first time he saw the
peak on the drive into Tucson from his home in Oregon
when he first accepted the job at Sungod. He had felt
compelled to slow down on the interstate as he passed
by the mountain. Both he and Carol looked closely at
the peak as they passed by. They vowed to visit the
oddly-shaped mountain in the near future. A few
months later he and Carol were climbing the mountain
on a regular basis.

Johnny remembered huffing and puffing
considerably after hiking only a few hundred yards
along the trail the first time he and Carol climbed the
peak. He remembered getting his second wind by the
time he reached the bottom of the cliffs. He really felt as

if he was accomplishing a great feat as he pulled himself up with the steel cables on the south side of the mountain on that first trip.

As he became an avid hiker of the many desert and mountain trails in the Tucson area, including Picacho Peak, he liked to think of his hiking trips as a metaphor for life. He believed in the old saying that enjoyment of the journey was more important than enjoyment of the destination or to paraphrase Emerson; wisdom is finding "the journey's end in every step of the road." For his first journey to the top of Picacho Peak, he assessed the journey and the destination as equally enjoyable and amazing.

He remembered the struggle to the top with a surprising change in scenery around every corner of the trail. He remembered standing on the top of the peak as if he was standing on the head of a pin floating above the desert. He remembered seeing everything for three hundred sixty degrees around down to the desert floor fifteen hundred feet below him.

He and his wife, Carol, revisited the peak once in the spring and once in the fall every year since that first hike until a few years before she and their son died. Nothing seemed the same after that.

Johnny recalled the chaos as he rushed to the scene of the accident that took the life of his wife and child five years earlier. Along with the car in front of her, Carol had pulled her mini-van off to the side of the road to let a massive dust storm pass over the interstate. An eighteen-wheeled truck and trailer traveling over the posted seventy five miles per hour speed limit hit the rear of the mini-van and propelled the van into the vehicle in front of it. The impact destroyed the two vehicles, their occupants, and Johnny Blue's life.

Johnny took six months leave of absence to recover, but never found the joy he had with his wife and son. He returned to work and went through the motions until cutbacks at the company allowed him to take early retirement. Now he spent his energy building a fortress of solitude out of straw in the desert.

"Checkpoint Hotel all secure," Johnny spoke into the radio as he locked the gate on Park Link Drive. "Picacho Patrol signing off."

CHAPTER 5

As the sun set on the western horizon, Johnny Blue drove his red pickup east on Park Link Drive and then a quarter mile down a rutty dirt road to the entrance of the ten acre ranch which he had recently purchased after selling his tract home in Marana. He stopped in front of the metal gate at the entrance to his driveway, straightened the "No Trespassing" sign, unlocked the gate, drove his pickup through the entrance, and then locked the gate behind him.

The main purpose of the gate and "No Trespassing" sign was to keep out the hunters, off road vehicle users, mountain bikers and hikers that invaded the untamed wilderness around Park Link Drive every weekend. Most of the land in the area was State Trust Land and open to the public for recreational activities. Even with the gate and fence surrounding his property people invaded Johnny's land on foot occasionally. At least the fence kept out the motorized vehicles. He drove a few hundred feet down the sandy single-lane road to the fifteen foot travel trailer he called home.

Park Link Drive was a dirt road that ran northeast off of the interstate just a few miles southeast of Picacho Peak and a few miles east of the town of Red Rock. The drive ran for eighteen miles from Interstate 10 until it intersected with Highway 79, a highway that ran from the northern Tucson area to the eastern edge of Phoenix. The drive was a shortcut used by travelers from Tucson headed to any of the eastern Phoenix suburbs or to Florence, the Pinal County seat. Travelers heading east on Interstate 10 used the road as a shortcut to the town of Oracle and its world famous

Biosphere north of Tucson or as a shortcut to the White Mountains in northeastern Arizona.

The land around Park Link Drive was nondescript except for the oddly shaped Owl Head Buttes and Tortolita Mountains on the southern side and the Picacho Mountain Range and lesser hills on the northern side. A group of independent minded individuals started buying up the land in the nineteen nineties. They plopped down manufactured homes and "No Trespassing" signs on ten acre or better lots. The new residents were seeking solitude from the meaningless drudgery of city life. Johnny purchased his lot near a small butte named The Huerfano on the northern side of the road.

He felt that the term Huerfano, a Spanish word meaning orphan, was an appropriate name for the land on which he planned to settle down for the rest of his life. Since his wife and child died, he felt like an orphan abandoned by his family. He had trouble relating to the rat-race style existence of his fellow workers when he worked at Sungod. He wanted more out of life, but not seeing anyway to get more, he wanted less.

His ten acre lot was located nine miles east of the interstate on the gentle southern slopes of the three hundred foot tall The Huerfano. Except for a small outcropping of rocks halfway up its western face, the orphan peak had long sloping sides that gave it pyramidal shape. Its slopes were covered with saguaro cacti and other Sonoran Desert plants.

A thirty foot tall metal windmill stood in the midst of the trees at the foot of the hill. Three silver colored metal legs angled out of the sandy soil and met underneath the fan-blades and rudder of the windmill. Metal brackets equally spaced along the height of legs braced them against each other. The mill was leftover from when the land was used to raise range cattle. A large cement tank used to provide water for cattle sat at the base of the windmill. Johnny had disconnected the pump from the windmill when he bought the property since he had no immediate intentions of raising cattle on his small plot of land.

He had positioned his trailer near the bottom of The Huerfano in an area covered with dense palo verde, mesquite, and ironwood trees. The travel trailer provided him temporary quarters until he could build his permanent home out of straw bales. He had already laid the foundation for the nine hundred square foot straw-bale house he planned to build.

Johnny parked his pickup truck in front of the entrance to his trailer. He grabbed the cardboard box of evidence out of the passenger's seat of the pickup and brought it inside. The one hundred twenty square feet of living space served Johnny well as temporary accommodations. A small couch at the back of the trailer served both as a bedroom and as a seat at the small table that served as a dining room and computer desk for his laptop. A small area in the front of the trailer included an electric refrigerator, a dual burner propane stove, and a stainless steel sink.

Even under the protection of the shade from the surrounding palo verde trees, the air inside the trailer was hot from the day's scorching sun. Johnny turned on the fan at the back of the trailer. He grabbed a towel and walked back outside to his makeshift outdoor shower consisting of a garden hose with an adjustable sprayer hung on a wooden post at the front of the trailer. He stripped off all his clothes, turned on the water and stepped under the spray.

As the spray from the water washed over him, he tried to wash the vision of Josephine Dvorak's face from his mind. Suddenly the vision of the face of the young woman was replaced with a vision of his wife Carol's own young face.

Melancholy and remembrance of the death of his wife took over his mind and body. He leaned his head against the wooden post and let the cold water run down his back. He felt himself sobbing uncontrollably for a few moments. He thought of his son Jerry. His son's innocent five year old smiling eyes and mouth stared at him in his mind. He tried to clear his mind and think of the present. He tried to think of his plans to build his house and how lucky he was to be living where he wanted to live in the desert. He quickly regained his composure and shut off the water. He dried himself with the towel and then wrapped it around his waist and walked back inside the trailer.

The breeze from the fan cooled his damp skin as he entered the trailer. In the many years he had lived in southern Arizona, he had never minded the heat. He felt comfortable with an inside temperature in the high eighties as long as at least a slight breeze was available to help his body cool itself. He kept the trailer windows open to let in the night air, which had already cooled considerably after the sunset.

Johnny sat down on the couch in front of his laptop computer and uploaded the pictures and the GPS waypoint he had collected at Checkpoint Golf. In his former life at Sungod Industries, Johnny was a Software Engineer that prided himself on his analytical mind. He knew there was nothing more exhilarating than solving a difficult problem through the use of the five pounds of gray matter enclosed in his skull. He also knew that there was nothing more frustrating and challenging than staring at a blank page of symptoms with no clue as to the cause of the problem.

"How did those crystals get in both places?" he asked himself. He swore that they were not there on his morning rounds but doubted that anyone would believe him or would care if he told them. It irritated him to think that people on the front line of defense of the country could sweep away suspicious activity so easily.

He wondered if it was laziness, ignorance, apathy, or all three that caused them to act the way they did. Were people too involved in their own petty lives to worry about the greater good, he wondered.

The sheriff wanted to write off the two deaths on the peak as an accident, but Johnny did not want to accept that until he knew more about the crystals and the tire tracks near the canal. At this point nothing linked the crystals to the two deaths in the park. The sheriff was probably right, he thought. The deaths were probably a case of overzealous hikers careless in their preparation for a hike in the desert heat.

Johnny displayed a topographic map of Picacho Peak and the surrounding area on his computer screen. He zoomed in on the area around the waypoint he had collected earlier. According to the map, the road near the waypoint led from the CAP canal to Wymola Bluff in the middle of the desert between the canal and the interstate. The road turned west at the bluff and continued to the same road Johnny drove on to get to the canal on his way to the Picacho Pumping Plant.

Anyone driving out to Checkpoint Golf would have to pass through the same unlocked gate Johnny passed through to get to Checkpoint Charlie. The only difference was that to get to Checkpoint Golf, one would turn east towards the bluff and then north to the checkpoint. Johnny wondered if the crystals in the two places were left by people or if there was not a more innocent explanation such as a bird with some digestion problems or possibly waste from an airliner. Birds and airliners did not leave tire tracks, he thought.

He picked up his cell phone and dialed the home number for a chemist friend of his named Jack Cecum. Jack and Johnny had worked together on a project when Johnny worked at Sungod Industries.

"Remember the time that I found that bug in your analysis software in time for you to make your testing deadline?" Johnny asked Jack Cecum after an exchange of pleasantries. "I need to cash in on that favor you owe me."

"Sure, what do you need; someone to help lift those straw bales up to the third floor?" Cecum asked.

"No. It's kind of hard to explain but I need you to do some chemical analysis for me," Johnny said. "Can you meet me for lunch tomorrow at that sports bar on Orange Grove Road around eleven thirty?"

"I'll meet with you, but I can't promise anything," Cecum replied.

Johnny hung up the phone and turned back to his computer screen. He looked again at the waypoint he had marked at Checkpoint Golf. He drew a line from the waypoint to the lava mound and then to Picacho Peak. He studied the line and realized that the mound was probably large enough to hide any activity at Checkpoint Golf viewed from the interstate. However, anyone hiking Picacho Peak would have a clear view of activity at the checkpoint.

CHAPTER 6

Johnny Blue awoke to the sound of Deputy Sheriff Juan Dugas pounding on the aluminum door on the side of his trailer on his ranch on Park Link Drive. Johnny answered the door dressed in a thin white undershirt and shorts and then stepped outside.

"I'd ask you in but there is not much room in there," Johnny said as he rubbed his eyes in the bright sunlight.

"That's all right," the deputy said. "I just came by to get that *evidence* you collected last night." The deputy made imaginary quotation marks with his fingers when he spoke the word "evidence." Johnny retrieved the photos and bag of crystals from the box inside the trailer.

"Let me ask you something," the deputy said as he took off his sunglasses. "You worked at Sungod for a while didn't you?"

"Ten years," Johnny replied.

"I understand this Josephine Dvorak worked there too," the Deputy continued. "Did you know her?"

"I saw her around a couple of times, but I didn't really know her," Johnny said.

"Did you recognize her yesterday?" the deputy asked.

"Yeah, I knew who she was," answered Johnny.

"I am just wondering why you didn't mention that to me yesterday," the deputy said as he stared straight into Johnny's eyes.

"I guess I was a little upset," replied Johnny without blinking. "I didn't know this girl that well but I had seen her around. It was a little upsetting to see her sitting there dead like that."

"All right. I'll buy that for now," the deputy said.

"What is the deal on these crystals you found?" he asked.

"I told you everything I know," Johnny replied. "I just found those two piles. They weren't there on my morning rounds so they looked suspicious. What do you think they are?"

"I'll tell you what I think," the deputy said moving closer to Johnny and pointing at Johnny's chest with his sunglasses. "I've got better things to do than spend my time investigating a couple of piles of blue crystals. These two deaths look like an accident and if you are yanking my chain with these crystals or there is something else going on here and you are involved, let me tell you I am going to come after you.

"I've got somebody out there shooting illegal aliens and I don't have time to deal with this shit. The State Police are going to do an autopsy on those bodies and if they died of natural causes the case is closed. I don't care how many blue crystals you find."

"Hey, I didn't ask to go out and find those two people dead in the desert," Johnny said. "As far as these crystals go, all I know is that the people around here are counting on me to recognize suspicious activity and report it to people like you. I hope these crystals aren't anything, but if they are something I hope we find out what the hell they mean before something like September 11th happens again. Now if you'll excuse me, today is my day off and I haven't had my breakfast yet."

Johnny retreated to the comfort of his trailer. The deputy walked a few hundred feet back up the sandy driveway to his car parked outside the property's entrance. Johnny grabbed an apple from the bag on his kitchen counter and sat down at the table to think about what the deputy had said. It sounded like the deputy was ready to close the case without looking at it, he thought. He had to find out what the crystals were about and whether they were related to the deaths or not.

Johnny put on a long-sleeved T-shirt, shorts and sandals and then walked out into the early morning sun. He took the Faithful Security Agency magnetic signs off the side of his pickup and threw them in the back of the vehicle. He started the engine and drove past the stack of straw bales underneath a blue tarp under a homemade ramada in front of his trailer.

He had recently purchased enough bales to build the nine hundred square foot house that he planned to use as his permanent residence. The bales lay on wooden pallets and were covered by a blue plastic tarp. Johnny hoped to have the structure built before the monsoon season began in earnest. Already he had the cement foundation laid down and only needed to lay down the bales, put up the roof, and plaster the walls. Then he could move his valuables out of his storage unit in Marana and begin enjoying his new straw-bale house. He just hoped that the monsoon rains would hold off for another week.

Johnny Blue drove thirty five miles from his ranch to Orange Grove Road in the city of Marana and found Jack Cecum waiting for him at a table in the sports bar at which they agreed to meet. Jack was of average height with an above average waist. His graying hair and wrinkled forehead betrayed the stress of working for over twenty years in the demanding field of chemical engineering at an aerospace and defense contractor.

The two men exchanged pleasantries and each ordered a cheeseburger basket and iced tea. Johnny explained the situation to Jack and asked him if he could look at the crystals to find out what they were.

"So you want me to smuggle some unknown substance into Sungod and use their equipment to figure out what it is?" Jack asked.

"You know as well as I that people walk in and out of that plant with stuff they aren't supposed to have all the time," Johnny replied. "I wouldn't ask if this wasn't serious and I didn't have anywhere else to go. What do you say?"

"All right," Jack replied. "But we're even after this."

"We're even," Johnny said as he passed the plastic bag of crystals to Jack under the table.

The waitress delivered the food and check in one motion. Johnny turned the conversation to Josephine. "Did you know her?" he asked.

"She was on the team for the proprietary project I am on," Jack replied. "I saw her in meetings, but nothing more than that. She said she was quitting so she could move back to Iowa and get away from the heat. Her husband was a carpenter and had some opportunity with an amusement park up there."

"Did the company have any problem with her leaving?" Johnny asked.

"What do you think that Sungod sent black helicopters out to shoot her down in the desert," Jack said. "You know people leave projects and the company all the time without any problems. You escaped didn't you?"

"Yeah, but I never worked on anything proprietary," Johnny replied. "I heard that security is pretty tight on those projects."

"They put on a pretty good show but I think it is all a load of crap," Jack replied. "There isn't anything different on those projects than any of the normal secret projects out there.

"There was a rumor going around that maybe she was pregnant. Her best friend took a year off to have a baby and one of the secretaries said Josephine was pretty enamored with the idea."

"Any idea how her husband felt about that?" Johnny asked.

"No one seemed to know much about him except that he worked out at that theme park in the Tucson Mountains," Jack replied.

"I've got to get back to work," he said.

Johnny threw a twenty dollar bill down on the table and shook Jack's hand. "You've got my number. I'd appreciate hearing about what you find out as soon as you can let me know," he said.

Outside the sports bar, Johnny could see thunderstorm clouds gathering on the western horizon. The monsoons were coming. It looked like he would not be able to start building his straw-bale house very soon.

He knew it was important to keep the straw bales dry to prevent rot once they were installed. He would have to let the monsoon pass through tonight and hope that the rest of the week was sunny so he could begin putting up the walls of his house.

Johnny tried to remember the moral of the fairy tale story of the three little pigs. In the fairy tale the first pig built his house of straw because it was the easiest thing to do and allowed him to spend the rest of the day playing.

Johnny tried to analyze his own motives for moving out into the desert and building a house of straw. Was he like the little pig that did not want any responsibility but just wanted to play all day without taking life seriously? Was he fooling himself into believing that a straw-bale house was some kind of rebellion against the societal norms in which people lived practically on top of each other in nearly identical ticky-tacky stucco houses?

Since Carol and Jerry died he had withdrawn from the world. Was that his true motive, to hide from the world so he could grieve in private over his loss and throw a pity-party for himself everyday? Was the desert or retirement life any place to hide? He had always thought of both places as barren without enough cover to hide anything. Maybe that was true and he needed to stop hiding and start living.

He tried to imagine what his life would be like once he built his house. Could he possibly live alone in the wilderness the rest of his life? His retirement income would certainly allow him to do so from a financial perspective; but what about from a human perspective? How much human interaction did he need to survive and be happy? Would going to town for supplies once a week be sufficient?

When he purchased the land, he thought of the ranch as a possible base from which to explore the country in his travel trailer. He had enough money to travel around the country if he wished. But he wondered if he would tire of traveling aimlessly on the road with no direction in his life.

Straw house construction had come a long way since the fairy tale of the three little pigs was first told. Properly constructed and maintained with straw-bale walls, stucco exterior and plaster interior, the modern straw house would remain water proof, fire resistant, and pest free throughout its lifespan. Johnny did not expect any big bad wolves to come around to huff and puff and blow his house down.

He pulled into one of the tire stores on Ina Road on his way back to the interstate. He recalled that a friend, Carlos Grijalva, had bought the store a few years earlier when he retired from Sungod Industries. Even with a population of over a half a million people the Tucson area had the atmosphere of a small town. Johnny seemed to meet someone he worked with at Sungod everywhere he went.

Johnny walked inside the small office on the side of the tire store. He found Carlos sitting with his feet up on his desk reading the local paper. After an exchange of preliminary greetings and catching up on each other's status as ex-Sungods, Johnny handed Carlos a printout of the picture of the tire tracks from Checkpoint Golf.

"I think someone may be trespassing on my property out there on Park Link," Johnny lied to prevent from having to explain the whole story to Carlos. "I took this picture of some tracks out there and was wondering if you could give me a clue as to what kind of vehicle would leave tracks like this."

"That's right you're building a house of straw out there aren't you?" Carlos replied with a smile as he studied the printout.

"It must have been a pretty heavy truck to make that deep of an imprint. Looks like a dual wheel pickup or truck. The wheels are pretty close together. I don't know maybe a water tanker or something."

"You mean like those trucks developers use to keep the dust down when they are clearing the land?" Johnny asked.

"Yes like that," Carlos replied. "Some of the farmers use something similar to keep the dust down when they are plowing. It really could be a number of vehicles though.

"What's this all about anyway? I see in the paper that the girl that died up on Picacho worked at Sungod. Does this have anything to do with that?"

"I don't think so," Johnny said. "Like I said, I think someone might be trespassing out there. I thought you might be some help and you have been." Johnny stood up to leave.

"Too bad about the girl," he said. "I guess she started working out there after you left. You didn't know her did you?"

"No, I was there before her time," Carlos said as he shook Johnny's hand. "You take care of yourself out in the desert. I worry about you."

Johnny walked out to his pickup and noticed that the clouds had darkened in the western sky. He hoped he could make it home without getting caught in a flash flood. He pulled out of the tire shop parking lot onto Ina Road. It took him a few years to get accustomed to Tucson's wide open skies compared to his home state of Oregon. In Oregon it rained everywhere at the same time for days and weeks on end. In Tucson it hardly rained at all except during the monsoon season, which generally ran from late June to late September. Thunderstorms would gather in isolated areas in the afternoon and drench several square miles with a cloudburst while leaving the rest of the Tucson area untouched. The storms never stayed in one place long and were easy to wait out.

In spite of the multitude of signs warning drivers not to enter flooded roadways, it seemed that with every storm at least one impatient driver would get their vehicle stuck trying to cross a flash flood. The problem became so bad that Arizona passed a law commonly known as "The Stupid Motorist Law." The law required motorists that got caught in flash floods due to their own stupidity to pay for any government assistance required to save them or their vehicles.

One of Johnny's favorite pastimes with his son Jerry had been to watch the storms pass over the valley below them from their backyard in the Tortolita Mountain foothills in the tract housing development they had lived in within the Marana city limits. The storms were much more violent than Oregon's steady rains. Johnny remembered Jerry squeezing his hand tighter with each bright flash of light and loud clap of thunder.

Johnny drove on to the interstate and headed northwest towards Park Link Drive. Raindrops speckled his windshield as he drove. By the time he reached the Red Rock exit the downpour slowed traffic on the interstate by thirty miles an hour. He took the exit and drove parallel to the interstate towards Park Link.

Johnny knew that there was no sense in turning down the drive towards his house. Park Link was certainly flooded and impassable and if it was not, then his driveway certainly was flooded. He planned to drive past the Park Link turnoff to Marcie's Restaurant to have a soda and catch up with Marcie while he waited the storm out.

Sheets of rain landed hard on his windshield as he approached the intersection with Park Link Drive. He could see that the dip in the road just before the intersection was flooded with dark brown muddy water foaming at the top as it rushed by. He pulled on to the shoulder and turned on his flashers to wait out the flash flood.

He recalled that his wife also pulled off to the side of the road that fateful day five years earlier when the dust storm overtook the interstate. He remembered getting the call at work about the accident. By the time he reached the accident scene, traffic had slowed to a crawl. He remembered parking on the shoulder of the highway a half a mile behind the accident and running towards the wreck. Mike Gerrity saw him and grabbed him around the waist to slow him down.

"You can't go near there," Johnny remembered Gerrity yelling over the sound of a large truck idling nearby. The wind was still gusty and dust and debris swirled all around them.

"I have to know if my wife was in that van," Johnny remembered yelling back.

He remembered the officer leading him to the ambulance which was still waiting for the bodies to be extracted from the twisted sheet metal. Gerrity sat Johnny down on the back bumper of the red box-shaped vehicle and asked the paramedic to give him a cup of water. "

"Sir," the officer said. "Do you know the license number of your wife's vehicle?"

Johnny remembered looking to the sky and trying to recall the license number. Finally it came to him and he repeated the numbers and letters to the deputy. Mike Gerrity shook his head and Johnny knew it was hers.

"What about my son?" Johnny remembered asking him. The officer just shook his head again and Johnny knew he had lost them both.

As he sat in his pickup waiting for the flood to clear, a white water tanker truck pulled off of Park Link Drive onto the road in front of him. The truck headed northwest on the road and away from Johnny. Johnny recognized the vehicle as the kind he and Carlos Grijalva had talked about. The truck went through another dip and sent curving streams of muddy water eight feet high into the air on each side of the road.

Johnny started his pickup, backed down the road twenty feet, and then pressed the acceleration pedal to the floor. Sprays of muddy water flew up on each side of the vehicle as he drove through the first flooded dip and then the second. He could see the brake lights on the vehicle as it reached the area around Marcie's Restaurant near the Picacho Peak entrance to the interstate around a mile ahead of him. Johnny saw the vehicle turn left and then disappear.

CHAPTER 7

When he arrived at Marcie's Restaurant near the Picacho Peak interstate on-ramp, Johnny circled the parking lot of the restaurant, gift shop and gas station. The white truck was not around. Johnny drove under the interstate to the south side of the freeway. He drove by the gift shop and the State Park entrance. There was no sign of the truck. He drove by the Indian trading post which had been out of business for a few years. There was no sign of the truck. He concluded that the truck must have driven onto the interstate and left the area.

Johnny drove back to the north side Frontage Road and parked his pickup in the parking lot of Marcie's Restaurant. The rain had stopped as quickly as it had started. He stepped out of the pickup and took in a deep breath of moist air. He enjoyed the fresh smell of the desert after a thunderstorm. He looked up at the jagged peak across the freeway. The thunderstorm had moved away to the west and the peak glistened in the bright sunlight.

Four large men wearing green camouflage outfits were in the process of exiting the restaurant as Johnny approached its entrance. One of the men held the door as Johnny entered. Johnny thanked the man towering above him. He had a three-day old growth of beard on his chin and smelled as if he had not had a change of clothes or a shower in several days.

"How are you doing, sugar?" Marcie Foster greeted Johnny as he entered the restaurant.

Marcie was a petite woman with an attractive face. Her short dark brown hair curling around the sides of her round face identified her as a mature woman that liked to look her best. Her natural good looks and bright smile had been the highlight of many a trucker's day over the years that her restaurant had serviced customers from the interstate and local farming community.

"I'm doing all right," Johnny said. He ordered and paid for a soda.

"What was all that about?" he asked indicating with a nod of his head the men getting into a green camouflage painted Ford Bronco in the restaurant parking lot.

"I guess they are part of one of those militia groups helping the farmers guard their ranches down around the border," Marcie said.

"What are they doing up this far north?" Johnny asked.

"They said they were just passing through on their way to Tombstone to join up with that newspaper editor that advertised in the Soldier of Fortune Magazine," Marcie said.

"It's been over a hundred and twenty years since the gunfight at the O.K. Corral, but it doesn't look like we've made much progress," Johnny said. "It's the wild, wild west all over again."

"I just hope they aren't involved in any of those killings of the border crossers," Marcie said.

"Me too," Johnny said. "Something has to be done about that. I heard there was another killing yesterday near Red Rock. I guess the sheriff is looking into it."

"I heard about you finding those bodies up on the peak," Marcie said as she sat down at a table near the front of the restaurant while Johnny filled his paper cup at the drink station.

"It was not a pretty sight," Johnny said. He told her about finding the bodies. He left out the part about the crystals. He thought it was better to wait until Jack got back to him in case they were nothing.

"I just saw a white tanker truck drive through a flash flood out on the frontage road," Johnny said. "Have you seen anything like that around here lately?"

"I don't remember seeing one," Marcie said. "We've been pretty slow so I would have noticed if they came in here. If they just used the gas station, maybe I would have missed them. What's this about?"

"Nothing, I just saw it high-tailing it through the floods down this way and thought you might have a special going on," Johnny said.

"You know you are the only one we treat special around here," Marcie said.

Marcie had inherited the restaurant when her husband died of a heart attack several years earlier. She had a house a few miles down the road near Red Rock. She retired to the house everyday after working twelve hours behind the counter. She had two employees, a Native American male named Carlos that cooked in the restaurant and his wife Shauna that worked the counter in the gift shop.

"I could use some special treatment about now," Johnny said.

"You need to get out more," Marcie replied. "You still haven't gotten over losing them have you? I don't think building a house of straw out in the wilderness is going to help. Do you?"

"Everything in its time," Johnny replied. "What about you? It's been ten years hasn't it? I don't hear any great stories of romance coming from you."

"First of all, you don't hear everything about me and second, I have my own little family right here in this restaurant and I meet new people everyday,"

Marcie replied. "Third, we are talking about you. So don't change the subject.

"You look tired. Have you been sleeping all right?"

"Not too well," Johnny replied. "Sorry about that crack. Finding that girl got me a little upset."

A dark blue late model large SUV pulled into the parking lot and skidded to a stop at the entrance to the restaurant. A white-haired man with a gray beard and a ponytail rushed through the door.

"There is a fire on the other side of the freeway," he said as he tried to catch his breath.

Johnny and Marcie stood up together and looked through the tinted windows of the restaurant towards the peak. A plume of black smoke billowed up over the interstate.

"Call the fire department," Johnny said to Marcie. "I'll go check it out."

Johnny rushed outside to his pickup. He examined the vehicle that the white-haired man had parked in front of the restaurant. The back window was covered with environmentalist bumper stickers protesting against bioengineered food. Johnny supposed that we would all be walking around naked gathering nuts and berries from the forest if this guy had his way.

Johnny drove under the interstate to the south side of the freeway. Black smoke poured out of the roof of the Indian trading post. Orange flames climbed up the giant polyurethane foam Indian standing guard in front of the building. Johnny looked around for a hose to douse the fire with, but he knew it was too late. He knew no one lived on the premises so at least he would not have to see any more dead bodies. A wall near the rear of the building fell away and Johnny saw what looked like a tanker truck melting in the flames. Debris from the roof covered the vehicle as flames and smoke encircled it.

A giant blast of orange fire shot out of the building towards Johnny. He felt as if he was moving in slow motion as the blast propelled him backwards. His feet left the ground and he felt himself toppling over backwards and then there was nothing. No sound. No light. Johnny's head fell dark and silent against the black asphalt pavement.

CHAPTER 8

Johnny Blue woke up in the Northwest Medical Center emergency room in Tucson near the eastern edge of the town of Marana. Even at thirty five miles away and in a different county, the hospital was the closest medical facility to Picacho Peak. Johnny was unconscious for nearly an hour before he groggily started coming around.

"What happened?" Johnny asked the young man with a white coat and glasses making notes on a clipboard. Johnny looked around him and saw that he was lying on top of white sheets on a hospital bed surrounded by a beige wrap-around curtain.

"Mr. Blue, I see you've decided to join us," replied Doctor Ron Smith.

"You are going to be all right. All your vital signs are normal," the doctor said. "It seems you had a little accident out at Picacho Peak. Can you tell me what you remember about what happened?"

"Mind if I listen in on this, Doc?" Deputy Juan Dugas said as he silently parted the wrap-around curtain and stepped in close to the bed.

"How are you doing there, sport?" the deputy said to Johnny.

"I've got conga drums playing in my head but other than that all right," Johnny replied. "I remember someone coming into the restaurant and saying that there was a fire across the freeway, so I headed over there. After that everything's pretty foggy."

The doctor and the deputy each made notes on their individual notepads.

"I want you to follow my finger with your eyes," Doctor Smith said. He held his right index finger six inches in front of Johnny's face. "It's a standard test to see if you have a concussion." The doctor moved his finger slowly to the right and then to the left. He intently watched Johnny's eyes move with the finger.

"Who is the president of the United States?" the doctor asked.

"George Bush," Johnny replied.

"Aw, but which one?" the doctor said with a chuckle.

"The second one, W," Johnny replied and all three men laughed.

"Looks good," Doctor Smith said as he made more notes on his clipboard.

"All right if I ask him a few questions?" Deputy Dugas asked the doctor.

"Don't be too rough on him. He'll be all right but he is going to have a hell of a headache," the doctor replied.

"I am going to want to keep you here for an hour or so just to make sure you are all right," the doctor said to Johnny. "Then I'll release you with a prescription for some pain killers. I'm going to make my rounds so talk to one of the nurses if you need anything." The doctor exited through the curtains and began consulting with the nurse behind the desk.

"So you don't remember much, huh?" Deputy Dugas asked.

"Nope. Just driving over there from the restaurant," Johnny replied.

"Any idea who the guy was that reported the fire?" the deputy asked.

"No. I assumed he was just off the interstate," Johnny said. "Marcie might know. She was there."

"She said the same thing as you," the deputy replied. "What happened before you arrived at the restaurant?"

Johnny groaned as he tried to sit up in the bed and then laid his head back down on the firm pillow. "I don't remember," he replied. "What's this all about?"

"There was a truck inside the trading post," the deputy said. "We think its gas tank exploded and that's what knocked you down. It was one of those water tanker trucks. Got any idea who it might belong to?"

"I don't know," Johnny replied. "Something about that sounds familiar, but I am having a hard time trying to think right now. My head is killing me."

The nurse arrived with two small white paper cups.

"Excuse me gentlemen," the nurse said. "Take these two pills Mr. Blue. These will help your headache."

Johnny took the cup with two blue pills, quickly emptied it into his mouth and then did the same with the cup of water. The nurse took the empty cups and walked away.

"Marcie said you were asking about a white tanker truck with dual wheels on the back when you came in tonight," the deputy said to Johnny.

"That's right," replied Johnny. "I was stuck behind a flash flood and the truck came out of nowhere off of Park Link. I just thought it seemed to be in an awful hurry."

"Did you get a look at who was driving?" the deputy asked.

"No. It was still pretty dark with the clouds overhead from the thunderstorm," Johnny replied. "Did you have any luck with the blue crystals yet?"

"The State Police are looking into them in Phoenix," the deputy said. "We might hear by the end of the week."

"What about out at the canal? Did you get out there today?" Johnny asked. His head felt better and he sat up on the bed.

"No. I was caught up with the investigation of the illegal alien killings near Red Rock all day," the deputy replied. "I guess the rain washed away any evidence out there. We have the pictures you took though. I am sure the State Police investigators can use them."

"That's right," Johnny said. "The tire tracks. The guy at the tire store said that they looked like they were made by a truck with dual rear wheels. Do you think there is a connection?"

"Why don't you let us worry about that?" the deputy replied. "Anything else you can remember about the guy that reported the fire?"

"Oh yeah," Johnny said. "I remember he had a bunch of anti-bioengineering and environmental activist type bumper stickers on the back of his Explorer. He doesn't seem to be so concerned about the environment to drive an economical car. Do you think he had anything to do with the fire?"

"Again, let us worry about that," the deputy said. "You need to get your rest and take care of yourself. Do you have someone to give you a ride back to your truck?"

Just then Marcie stepped within the confines of the curtains with a small bouquet of flowers.

"I think I do," Johnny said smiling.

"I'll leave you two alone," the deputy said as he started to walk through the part in the curtains. "Let me know if you remember anything that might be useful."

"Wait," Johnny said and then grabbed his head in pain. "It may be nothing but there was a group of those militia men leaving Marcie's restaurant when I arrived."

"Is that right?" the sheriff asked Marcie.

"Yes," Marcie said. "There were four of them all in camouflage outfits and driving a camouflaged Bronco. They said they were going down to Tombstone to see that newspaper editor that ran the ad for them to help the ranchers patrol their land."

"Okay thanks for the information," the deputy said. He made more notes on his pad as he walked through the part in the curtains.

"How you doing, hon'?" Marcie asked as she leaned over and gave him a kiss on the cheek. "Are you going to be all right?"

"Aside from a massive headache, I think I'll be fine," Johnny replied.

The two reviewed the course of events of the evening. Marcie told Johnny that she heard the explosion and drove over to find him lying on the ground. The paramedics arrived a short time later and took him away. The trading post was so engulfed in flames by the time the firefighters arrived that they had to let it burn completely to the ground before extinguishing the blaze. All that was left of the foam Indian out front was the lower half of his legs from the knees down.

"I thought you might need a ride home," Marcie said.

Behind Marcie, Doctor Smith appeared clipboard in hand and said, "I agree with your diagnosis young lady."

He turned to Johnny and talked him through the concussion test again. He tore a small piece of paper off of his clipboard and explained the prescription to Johnny. "Two four hundred milligram pills every four hours and you should have no trouble with your headaches," he said. "Let me know if you do. Just check out with the nurse before you leave."

"Why don't you bring the car around?" Johnny asked Marcie. "I want to have a word with the Doc here and then I'll meet you out front." Marcie picked up the bouquet and walked towards the exit.

"Listen Doc," Johnny said. "Did you hear about the couple that died on Picacho Peak over the weekend?"

"The paper said they died of heat stroke," Doctor Smith replied.

"Yeah that is what's bothering me," Johnny said. "They were only out there for a few hours and they had four bottles of water with them. I know it was hot, but have you ever heard of heat exhaustion setting in that fast."

"It's possible," Doctor Smith replied. "Heat is a funny thing. It affects each individual differently. Some people have a high tolerance for it; some don't. A lot depends on their metabolism and how fast their kidneys process liquids in the body. The body needs fluids to keep it cool and if the kidneys process the fluids into urine too fast, it's easy to become dehydrated and the body overheats."

"I understand these people were in pretty good shape and hiked the peak before," Johnny said. "Does that make any difference?"

"It might," the doctor replied. "But you have to understand that once heat exhaustion starts to set in, it affects the mind and people don't always act rational.

People have been known to sit down to rest in the sun and never get back up."

"That's exactly how these two looked," Johnny said. "It looked like they just sat down and died."

"It was pretty hot out there," the doctor replied as Marcie walked up behind him. "I think you need a couple of days of rest and relaxation. Take it easy and don't worry about what happened out there."

After checking out with the nurse behind the desk, Marcie and Johnny walked out of the hospital into the night. "I'll be riding in style tonight," Johnny said as he approached Marcie's late model Cadillac. "I sure appreciate you coming to get me."

"Nothing but the best for you," Marcie replied. "How's your head?"

"Thick as ever," Johnny said. "The headache seems to be subsiding. What do you think about that truck they found in the trading post?"

"I don't know," Marcie said. "I hadn't seen it around before. That place went out of business three years ago and as far as I knew no one had been around it since. I guess I was wrong."

"I just wonder what is going on out there," Johnny said.

They stopped at the pharmacy to fill Johnny's prescription. The pharmacist explained the cautions and side effects of the medicine, including drowsiness. Johnny asked the pharmacist about possible dehydration with the medicine.

"It shouldn't be a problem with these pills," the pharmacist replied.

"What kind of medicines do you have to worry about that with?" Johnny asked.

"There are a lot out there," the pharmacist said. "Diuretics are the worst though. They make your kidneys produce more urine and literally suck the liquids right out of your system. They make you urinate a lot. Why? Are you having trouble with dehydration?"

"Just curious," Johnny said and then he walked out of the pharmacy.

Marcie spent the thirty five minute drive back to the trading post trying to convince Johnny to spend the next two days in bed. She extracted a promise from him to take it easy.

"That girl you found still has you shook up doesn't she?" Marcie said as she drove past the Red Rock exit on Interstate 10.

"I just can't believe anyone could die of heat exhaustion that quickly," he said.

"Hey it happens," Marcie said. "Just let it go for a couple of days. Let the cops do their tests and see what they come up with."

"I guess you are right," Johnny said as Marcie pulled her Cadillac into the parking lot next to his car. The light of the half-full moon shone down on the charred remains of the trading post giving it a ghostly glow. Johnny could see the bottom half of the foam Indian's legs standing in the moonlight just as Marcie described them.

"I am going to sit right here and follow you out of this parking lot to make sure you don't go snooping through that debris," Marcie said as she saw where Johnny's gaze had turned.

Johnny leaned his face in close to Marcie's ear and whispered, "You are quite a woman. I owe you for this so just name your price."

"Go on and get in that pickup before I think of a price you aren't ready to pay," Marcie said with a chuckle.

Johnny got into his pickup, started the engine, turned on his headlights, made a U-turn and drove through the underpass with Marcie driving close behind. The two vehicles turned east on Frontage Road towards Park Link Drive. When they reached the turnoff, the two friends waved at each other as Johnny turned east towards his home and Marcie continued on towards her house in Red Rock.

As he got out of his pickup to open the gate that led to his property, Johnny felt the effect of the pain killer starting to wear off and his head began to throb. When he got inside the trailer he swallowed two more pills with two gulps of water from a squeeze bottle and then lay down on the couch in the rear of the trailer and fell fast asleep with the image of Josephine Dvorak's face in his mind.

CHAPTER 9

Johnny awoke with the veins in the temples of his head pounding with each beat of his heart. He grabbed his head with both hands and walked to the kitchen at the front of his travel trailer. Johnny grabbed the bottle of pain relievers the pharmacist had given him, awkwardly fumbled two pills out of the bottle, and then swallowed them with two gulps of water from the squeeze bottle on the counter. He laid back down on the couch. The image of Josephine Dvorak's red parched face appeared in his head as he fell asleep.

He woke up two hours later to the sound of his cell phone ringing.

"Hello sugar," Marcie's voice came through the receiver. "How is that headache you got last night?"

"Still pounding," Johnny replied even though the throbbing in his temples had subsided somewhat. "What's up?"

"The State Police have been around asking questions about you," Marcie said. "I thought you might like to know."

"What kind of questions?" Johnny asked.

"Who your friends are, where you live, that kind of thing," Marcie said.

"I hope you answered their questions," Johnny said. "I don't have anything to hide. The sooner they stop looking at me, the sooner they might find out what is going on out there."

"Are you keeping that place cool and staying in bed like I told you?" Marcie asked.

"I have the fan blowing through the place. I have been sleeping all day," he replied. He looked out the side window of the trailer and noticed Officer Mike Gerrity walking around outside near his tarp covered straw bales. "The State Police are here. Got to go," he said into the cell phone and then hung up.

He stepped out of his trailer on to the sandy desert floor. "What brings you out this way, Mike," Johnny asked. He walked towards the officer and shook his hand.

"Just came out to see how your retirement is coming along Johnny," the officer replied with a smile. "This is quite a place you have here. You can see the Owl Heads, the Tortolitas, and the Catalinas to the east and Picacho, Ragged Top, and the Silverbells to the south and west."

Johnny appreciated someone recognizing the quality of the property he had chosen to reside on and said so. "It took me a while to find the perfect spot where I could get the views I want, but this is it," Johnny said as he scanned the horizon in all directions with his outstretched arm. "It is a special place."

"The sheriff tells me you've been involved in quite a bit of trouble the last few days," the officer said as he adjusted his hat to allow the sun to shine on his red face.

"I don't know if involved is the right word," Johnny said. "Why don't you sit down here in the shade and let's talk about it?" Johnny pointed to the white plastic patio chairs sitting in the shadow of his trailer and sat down.

"How's your head?" the officer asked as he sat down in the chair next to Johnny.

"I think it will be all right," Johnny said. "The pain pills help, but they make me sleepy."

Johnny recounted the events of the previous two days and told him about the blue crystals, the tire tracks, and the tanker truck. He told the officer about the recurring image of the face of his former co-worker in his mind. He expressed his disbelief at the two hikers dying so quickly.

"I just wish I knew what was going on around here," Johnny said.

"This sheriff thinks you might be another Richard Jewell, the security guard that seemed to be involved in the Olympic bombings a few years ago. He thinks you might be trying to make a name for yourself by causing problems and then solving them," the officer said. "You seem to be the only common link between the incidents."

"If I remember right, Richard Jewell was never linked to the bombing and was never charged with any wrong doing," Johnny said. "That said, I am no Richard Jewell. I wish to hell I'd never seen any of that stuff out there. I just took this job because it was part-time, brought in a little extra money, and it was close to home. I thought, maybe just maybe, I could help protect this country from a terrorist attack or at least reduce the chance that anyone with ill-intentions would try anything along the canal on the weekends."

"I am on your side," the officer said. "I am just telling you what the sheriff said. You have really been a big help in bringing this information to our attention. Just let the professionals handle this.

"Why don't you take the next couple of days and work around your place here? It'll keep you out of trouble.

"Take my card and if you think of anything that needs to be looked into, call me and I'll look into it." Officer Gerrity handed Johnny his card.

"The way these pills are knocking me out, I won't be going anywhere or thinking about anything," Johnny replied. "Besides just look around here. What reason do I have to leave?"

The two men shook hands and the officer walked back down the driveway to his car and drove away.

Johnny gathered up his soap and bottle of shampoo, stripped off his clothes and stepped underneath the cool spray of the custom showering stall next to his trailer. He could feel the blood rushing through his temples as he let the cool water run over his head and down the rest of his body.

The image of Josephine's face appeared in his mind until he could bear it no longer. There was no way he was going to spend the day alone with that face popping into his head every five minutes. He dried himself off, wrapped a towel around him and entered the trailer to get dressed to go into town.

CHAPTER 10

As he loaded the front seat of his pickup with a fresh bottle of water, GPS unit and digital camera, Johnny thought about the information he got from the doctor and the pharmacist the day before. He wanted to find out more about death by heat stroke and the diuretics the pharmacist mentioned. Had he not sworn to live a life of simplicity, he would have had a phone line connected to his property and could search the Internet for more information. Instead he was forced to drive to the nearest library in Marana.

Near the library was the Laundromat that he used to wash his clothes since his life of simplicity prevented him from owning a washer and dryer. He could kill two birds with one stone by driving into town and washing his clothes while he used the services of the library. He loaded his mesh laundry bag full of dirty clothes into the back of his pickup, sat down in the driver's seat and drove down his sandy driveway towards Park Link Drive.

Johnny turned right on Park Link and drove down the hard packed sandy road towards Interstate 10. A white pickup passed by from the direction of the interstate and Johnny recognized the Red Ruby Real Estate logo on the driver's door. He hoped that the driver was using the road as a shortcut to Highway 79 and not looking for another area of the desert to desecrate with a Red Ruby Real Estate Master Planned Community.

Johnny knew that most of the land along the drive was either State Trust Land or occupied by self-described antisocial landowners like himself. It would not be the first time Red Ruby Real Estate used its political clout to acquire government land, clear it of all its natural beauty and then put up a golf resort for wealthy retirees to congregate at during the winter.

Like many of his neighbors Johnny moved to the Park Link Drive area to find solitude and simplicity in his life. All he asked for was a few acres he could use as a retreat from the workaday world and the hustle and bustle of everyday living. A Red Ruby Real Estate development in the area would destroy that dream.

Johnny knew that the developer's effort to put up a resort in the area had already been thwarted once by the cotton farmers and cattle ranchers on the south side of the freeway. He just hoped that the developer did not decide to move his efforts to the north side. A resort on the south side would be far enough away to limit the impact of increased population and traffic near Johnny's ranch. Still, Johnny could see the traffic increasing on Park Link Drive to the point where they would have to pave it. He felt that a Red Ruby Real Estate development within even twenty miles of his residence would be intolerable.

He knew that the drought of the last decade almost forced the farmers to give in to the developer's demands. He knew that the CAP water he protected on the weekends had a hand in saving both the farmers land and the area around Johnny's lot from the invasion of the developer. He wondered if he was fighting a losing battle. If the current wave of urban sprawl would eventually overtake all of southern and central Arizona until Tucson and Phoenix became one giant two hundred fifty mile wide and two hundred mile long metropolis.

Greedy developers were not the only antagonist confronting the cotton farmers. Johnny had read in the newspaper about how the cotton farmers in the area were among the first to grow a new biotech pest resistant version of their crop. The bioengineered cotton grown by the farmers contains a bacterial gene that enables the plant to make its own insecticide. The new strain of cotton was eagerly adopted by Arizona growers seeking relief from the pink bollworm, a boll-munching caterpillar.

Fearing the crops would lead to a race of super-bugs as the pests adapted to the new version of the cotton, environmental activists had staged several protests over the previous half decade. The previous year tens of thousands of dollars worth of damage to farm equipment had been blamed on eco-terrorists although no group had claimed responsibility and the perpetrators were never caught. Protesters, such as Greenpeace, used less violent means to get their point across by trying to block the import of Arizona cotton in European countries.

Johnny felt that the farmers were in a "damned if they do and damned if they don't" position. The attack of the voracious bollworm in the nineteen nineties severely threatened their livelihoods, so they introduced the new biotech strain of cotton to save their farms. Then a drought over the next few years threatened their farms again and they saved themselves by accepting CAP water. All the while they were being portrayed by the liberal press and environmentalists as destroying the land and the environment.

The pressure from developers for the farmers to give up their land to turn it into housing tracts was disheartening to Johnny. Not to mention that, in Johnny's opinion, the last thing Arizona needed was another golf resort for the idle rich. The term "snowbird" was often used as a term of derision by the locals around the Tucson area. Every year the area was invaded by taller and longer motor homes driven by older and slower senior citizens out to spend their children's inheritance. The roads and other infrastructure strained to accommodate the additional winter traffic and the local residents became more frustrated every year. Building another golf resort would only encourage more snowbirds to visit the area and frustrate the local residents.

Johnny pulled into the parking lot of the Laundromat in what he called "old town" Marana. The old town area reflected Marana's history as a small rural agricultural community. The area consisted of a single gas station with a convenience store, a diner style restaurant, a Laundromat, a chamber of commerce office, a small post office, a park with a swimming pool, and an elementary school.

An abandoned grocery store stood off on a side street as testament to the growth of the town away from the "old town" western agricultural area to the "new town" eastern commercial districts near the Tucson metropolis. Several major chain department stores and grocery stores, as well as every other type of business a thriving community demanded, sprung up on the eastern city limits away from the city center allowing the farmers to keep their small town atmosphere separate from the urban sprawl taking over the city.

As he loaded his entire wardrobe into a single washer, Johnny waved to Sherry and Frank, the Laundromat's husband and wife owners who were folding clothes in the back room. He walked to the back of the Laundromat and purchased his usual single-load box of detergent from the proprietors. The couple had sold their farm to their son a few years earlier and started the small laundry business to keep themselves busy. They were in their late sixties but years of hard work and struggle in the desert made them look older. Their eyes smiled as they focused on folding the clothes a customer had dropped off earlier in the day.

"How is retired life in the laundry business?" Johnny asked.

Both husband and wife smiled and said in unison, "We are really cleaning up in here."

Johnny laughed even though he had heard the joke once a week for the last two months. "How is your boy doing with your farm?" he asked.

"If he can keep the pinkos from burning up his equipment, he might get a crop to market," Frank said. "Not to mention the CAP people can't keep the water running to the fields and the wetbacks keep leaving garbage all over the farm as they pass through in the middle of the night."

"Sounds like he's getting it from all sides," Johnny said. "Has there been more trouble with the environmentalists?"

"Not yet, but I feel it coming," Frank said as his wife tried to calm him down. "You know he lost a couple of trucks when those longhairs set fire to them back in January.

"A few weeks later he caught one of them pouring poison in the irrigation ditch along the canal. They didn't have enough to do any damage, but who knows what they'll try next. It was some old white-haired guy with a ponytail driving one of those big late model SUVs. I guess he can afford to terrorize someone trying to make an honest living. I think they arrested him and gave him a fifty dollar fine.

"I heard another illegal got shot out there by Red Rock. The S.O.B. had no business out there by the irrigation canal. They say the police found one of his compatriots and he said there were another two dozen illegals with them. They just up and disappeared. I hope to God someone took them back across the border where they belong."

"I've got to get over to the library before it closes," Johnny said. "I'll be back to start the dryer in a few minutes."

"We'll watch them for you and put them in the dryer when they are ready," Sherry said from across the room.

Johnny dumped the blue crystals of detergent into his wash and felt the temples in his head throb. He reminded himself to call Jack Cecum to check on his analysis after he got home. As he walked across the empty street to the library, he popped two pills in his mouth and swallowed them with a gulp of water from his squeeze bottle.

Johnny greeted the elderly librarian, Joanne Masters, with a smile as he entered the small one room library. Joanne's husband had died several years earlier just after they sold their farm and bought a motor home for traveling around the country. After her husband died, she sold the motor home and bought a small house near the old town area of Marana and then dedicated herself to bringing her hometown a library. Although funded by the government, the building and everything in it belonged to Joanne and everyone in the area knew it.

"Mind if I use your computer, Miss Masters?" Johnny asked. He surveyed the empty library consisting of four walls lined with bookshelves. Four more bookshelves, two computers and a single table with four chairs filled the room in the area between the walls.

"It's Mrs., thank you," the librarian said politely as she set down the Greek architecture book she was reading. "Those computers belong to the city of Marana not me and yes, you may use one of the library's computers as soon as you fill out the sign-up sheet."

"All right, Mrs. Masters. Thank You," Johnny said. The two friends chuckled softly.

"What brings you down here?" the librarian asked.

"Just the weekly check of my email and to look up some information on the Internet," Johnny replied.

"Anything I can help you with?" she asked.

"Do you know anything about diuretics?" he said.

"Assuming the word comes from the Greek terms *dia* meaning through and *ourein* meaning urinate I would say diuretics are some kind of drug that makes one urinate," she said. "We have a book on medicines over here if you would like to look through it."

"I'll stick to the Internet," Johnny replied as he sat down at the computer terminal. "I'd hate to hurt my wrist flipping through the pages of an actual book."

"I'll look for you," Joanne said as she walked out from behind the desk to the reference shelf. She picked up the Physician's Desk Reference. "What do you need to know about them?"

"Just general information," Johnny replied as he brought up his email account on the screen. He weeded out a dozen spam messages and was left with one email. It was from Jim Morrison a guy he used to play tennis with occasionally. He pulled up the email and read,

"Johnny,

I am looking for someone to play tennis with on Wednesday. I've got a court reserved at the club for 6 p.m. Let me know if you are interested.

My old playing partner is moving back to Iowa next week.

Let me know if you can make it.

-- Jim"

Johnny wondered if the former playing partner could possibly be Larry Dvorak. He wondered how many people in the Marana area were moving back to Iowa. The coincidence would be unusual since the town of Marana was such a small place.

The date on the email was from the previous Friday, two days before Johnny found the body of Larry Dvorak on Picacho Peak. It was Tuesday afternoon and Johnny could feel the pain pills starting to kick in. He felt drowsy. He doubted his head would be in any shape to play tennis the next evening, but the fact that Morrison may know Larry Dvorak intrigued Johnny.

He accepted the invitation to play with a short reply to the email. He let Morrison know that he would meet him at the tennis club at six the next evening.

"Is there any specific diuretic you are interested in?" the librarian asked Johnny from behind her desk.

"I was looking for something that might cause dehydration in a matter of hours," Johnny said.

"Now why in the world would you want to find something like that?" the librarian asked.

"I'm just doing some research for a friend," Johnny said. He brought up his favorite search engine on the screen and typed in the words *diuretics* and *dehydration* and then pressed the search button.

"This isn't about those poor people you found on the peak is it?" she asked.

"You've heard about that have you?" Johnny replied.

"Not much goes on around in this area that I don't hear about one way or another," she said. "I was sorry to hear about the young couple and sorry you had to find them. How are you dealing with seeing them like that?"

"I am handling it all right," he said.

He returned his gaze to the computer screen. He clicked on the first link to find a general description of diuretics and a list of common ones used. Lasix, used to treat high blood pressure and swelling due to excess water, was listed as the most common and most powerful. Johnny wrote down as much information as he could on a piece of scratch paper.

"How about looking up Lasix for me?" Johnny asked the librarian and then returned to his reading.

He found an article that said that aside from its prescribed medical uses, some athletes like weight lifters and wrestlers used the drug to quickly lose water weight before a weigh-in and to remove excess water from their body so their muscles would be more prominent when they posed. He also found several pharmaceutical sites willing to sell the drug without a prescription.

"I found it if you want to look," Joanne said.

Johnny leaned over her desk to read the information. The book said that the drug took affect in less than an hour and caused the body to produce and eliminate more urine than normal. It also said that the drug may cause the body to lose too much potassium. It said that users should eat foods high in potassium like bananas, raisins and orange juice to replenish the loss of the mineral. Johnny wrote down the information on the scrap paper and stepped back from the desk. He yawned and stretched his arms over his head.

"Are you all right?" Joanne asked. "You look tired."

"I am taking some medicine that makes me drowsy," Johnny said. "I'll be all right."

"Not this stuff, I hope," she replied. "You don't have high blood pressure do you?"

"No, it is something else," Johnny said. "I bet my clothes are done, so I guess I will head home. Thanks for your help Miss Masters. I mean Mrs. Masters."

"I will see you next week," the librarian replied. "Take care of yourself and get some rest."

Johnny walked across the empty street to the Laundromat. His clothes were already washed, dried, folded and laid out on the counter near the entrance. Johnny stuffed the clothes into his mesh laundry bag and walked towards the back room. Sherry lifted her eyes from the book she was reading as she rocked back and forth in a rocking chair.

"Where is Frank?" Johnny asked.

"He just stepped out for a smoke," Sherry said.

"Here is a couple of dollars for the dryer and folding," Johnny said as he set three one dollar bills on the counter. He rubbed his temples and frowned.

"Are you all right?" Sherry asked. "You look tired."

"I'm fine," Johnny said. "I was wondering about what Jack said earlier about the CAP water. Have they been cutting water off from your old farm?"

"They cut it off three times over the last three weeks," Sherry replied. "Our boy scheduled delivery of the water like usual, but when it didn't come; the CAP people told him there was some kind of contamination problem with the water coming out of the Red Rock Pumping Plant. They wanted to let it clear before anyone used the water."

"Did your boy say what the contamination was from?" Johnny asked.

"No he didn't," Sherry said. "I guess the CAP people would know."

"Do you remember the dates they refused to deliver the water?" Johnny asked.

"Yesterday morning for one," Sherry replied. "And I think maybe it was on the previous Mondays too. That's strange. I never realized that they shut it down on the same days. Maybe that's when they did their testing or maybe that's when our boy ordered it for delivery."

"Did they ever deliver the water?" Johnny asked.

"Two days later they did," Sherry replied. "But now my boy is seeing some of his cotton fields dying and he can't figure out why. They've got the Department of Agriculture out taking samples, but the tests aren't back yet."

Johnny thanked her for her help and walked back to his car. He knew that the testing on the CAP water was continuous and that a contaminant would have to approach an unsafe level for CAP to shutdown delivery.

The canal was not like a flowing river that farmers could just tap anytime they wanted to. They had to order their water several days in advance and the CAP pumping plant would dump the water into their irrigation canals at the appropriate time. From there it was up to the controllers of the local irrigation district to ensure all the proper gates in their irrigation ditches were open to guide the water to the appropriate fields.

CAP monitored the quality of its water but was not in the business of treating it. They let the end users take care of water treatment and only guaranteed delivery, not treatment. CAP monitored for contaminants and let the end user decide if they wanted to accept contaminated water or not. Unlike municipalities which sent the CAP water through a treatment facility, the farmers took the CAP water directly into their own irrigation ditches without treatment. This was deemed acceptable by the EPA Clean Water Act since CAP monitored the water before delivery and the farmers could refuse delivery if there was anything wrong with the water.

Johnny had not been told about the water being contaminated over the previous weeks. He figured that was probably because he was only a part time contract employee and the problem seemed to clear up before he started his weekend shift. He saw the lack of data passed on to people like himself as a problem. If the people on the front lines were given more information they might be able to put some of the pieces together and understand what was going on better. He wondered if the blue crystals he found could have anything to do with the shutdown of the CAP system.

He knew that lack of proper communication was a systemic problem with security outfits everywhere, just as it was in the days and months leading up to the September 11, 2001 tragedy. Isolated events, like pieces of a jigsaw puzzle, occurred and were reported by the people on the front line, but no one at the top seemed to be putting the pieces together to get the big picture. He wondered if anyone reported the incidents, including the crystals he found, to the Homeland Security Department or were the State Police and Sheriff's Office working in a vacuum.

Johnny's temples began to throb again as he drove northwest on the interstate towards Park Link Drive. He tried to make a mental note to call Mike Gerrity about the Homeland Security angle, but his head hurt so bad he was not sure if the note stuck. He popped two more pills in his mouth and swallowed them with water from his squeeze bottle.

He turned northeast onto Park Link Drive; the camouflage painted Bronco he saw the day before came turned off of Park Link on to Frontage Road towards Marcie's Restaurant. Johnny felt his head pound again as he tried to make another mental note. He thought the militia men were headed to Tombstone. He wondered why they were still in this area. Maybe they camped out overnight on some of the farmland around Red Rock or on the State Trust Land along Park Link Drive.

As he got out of his pickup to open the gate to his property, he found a yellow note taped to the gate. He stuck it in his pocket without reading it. By the time he pulled up to his trailer, he was drowsy again. He grabbed his laundry bag, entered the trailer, laid down on the bed and fell asleep.

CHAPTER 11

Johnny Blue lay on his bed half awake with visions of circus clowns dancing in his head. He suddenly realized that his cell phone was ringing, its programmable ringer set to circus music. He grabbed the phone from the table above his bed and felt the veins in his temples expand and contract with the rapid beating of his heart.

"This is Jack Cecum," the voice came through Johnny's cell phone. "I have some information on those crystals you had me look at."

"Hang on a second," Johnny said as he sat up on the bed and swung his legs underneath the table. He noticed that the clock in the kitchen displayed the time as 7:45 P.M. He also noticed that the evening light was fading. He had been asleep only a few hours although it felt like more. He grabbed his pen and the scratch paper he took from the library. "Sorry about that. What did you find out?"

"It's an herbicide known as Nectubethiuron," Jack said. "They use it to clear brush and grass off of rangeland. It's used pretty commonly in areas that don't have food crops. It can also be applied around airports and roadsides, that kind of thing."

Johnny felt his temples throbbing as he wrote down the information. "You didn't get all that from your chemical analysis did you?" Johnny asked.

"No. I took the liberty of doing a little research on the Internet," Jack replied. "I found a case in New Mexico a few years back where the government helped a private landowner spray his land with the herbicide using crop duster airplanes. Apparently they sprayed during the monsoon season and the rain washed the herbicide into some nearby irrigation canals. It wiped out several hundred acres of cotton before they realized what was going on."

"How do they apply this stuff?" Johnny asked.

"For large areas they drop pellets from airplanes," Jack said. "It can be dissolved in water and used as a spray to touch up specific areas like around sidewalks also."

"Sounds like you did a lot of work," Johnny said. "I appreciate your help. I don't know what all this means, but I appreciate your help."

"Do you think this has anything to do with the death of Josephine?" Jack asked.

"I don't know," Johnny said. "I just don't know."

Johnny hung up the phone and took two more pills. His head was throbbing and he could not bear to look at the notes he took. He remembered his concern about notifying the Homeland Security Department. It was eight o'clock in the evening. He decided it was not too late to call Mike Gerrity.

"Mike this is Johnny Blue," Johnny spoke into his cell phone when the officer answered. "Sorry to bother you at this hour. Do you have a few minutes to talk?"

"What's on your mind Johnny?" the officer asked.

"I just heard through the grapevine today that CAP has cut the water off from some of the farmers the last three Mondays in a row," Johnny said. "I just wanted to get your take on whether all these incidents don't add up to calling in the Homeland Security Department. I am worried about those crystals being so near the canal, not to mention an arson and two deaths. I am not convinced that all these things are not related. For all I know there may be something out there someone else knows about that would tie all of them together."

"I hadn't heard about the CAP incidents but I'll check into them," the officer said. "As far as the Homeland Security Department goes, I'll have to think about it. There is a certain process we have to go through to call them in. I'll run it by my supervisor tomorrow."

"All right," Johnny said and then he pressed the disconnect button on his cell phone.

His temples throbbed again. He laid down on his bed and fell asleep.

CHAPTER 12

Johnny Blue awoke at twelve o'clock noon on the Wednesday after he had found two dead bodies near the base of Picacho Peak. He was a morning person and normally got up a few hours earlier, but the pain pills and headache he had suffered for the last few days caused him to sleep in.

He drank water from his squeeze bottle to reduce the dehydration he felt weakening his body. His head felt normal, so he decided to forgo ingesting the last two pain pills the doctor had prescribed for him. The events of the previous three days clouded his mind and spirit.

He could clearly hear the negative tapes in his head begin their chant. "Who are you to call the police and tell them to bring in the Homeland Security Department? You probably missed those crystals on your first round. You aren't qualified to even watch a canal part time. Why can't you let the professionals do their work? You just have to stick your nose into everything don't you?"

He knew that he needed to re-center his thoughts. He opened the meditations sound file on his laptop computer using a standard sound recorder program and then pressed the play button. He sat down on a white plastic patio chair outside his trailer. He set his feet down flat on the sandy ground, straightened his back, put his hands on his knees, and then closed his eyes.

Carol's voice came through his computer's speakers and wafted through the open window of the trailer as if she was speaking to him from the dead.

"You are a good person. You are smart. You have an instinct for what is right. People depend on you to fight for what is right. You are strong. You are intelligent. You have a good heart. You make me laugh."

Johnny smiled at the last sentence as the positive affirmations continued. The recording grew out of therapy sessions he went to when he had a problem with depression when the stress of working at Sungod Industries overwhelmed him early in his career. The sessions revealed that years of mental and emotional abuse at the hands of his alcoholic father had shattered his self-confidence. It was as if he had a little tape player in his head constantly playing negative putdowns of himself in his own voice.

He made several attempts at trying to control his thoughts and keep the negative tapes from playing in his head, but he always lapsed back into letting them control his attitude towards life. He had tried meditating in silence every morning but all that did was clear his mind of everything but the sound of the negative tapes.

Finally Carol suggested making his own sound recordings and listening to them while he meditated. She suggested that he might be able to record over the negative tapes with positive affirmations about himself. Carol made a recording of her thoughts on how she saw her husband and Johnny used them to try to record over the negative tapes in his head.

Johnny remembered that after several weeks of playing the tapes in the morning and at night before he went to bed a noticeable change came over him. The anger left his body and mind. He felt a warm spot grow in his chest just below his heart. For the first few days he wondered if the warmth was caused by a physical ailment such as a tumor. After a while he grew accustomed to the warm spot and his focus returned to the activities of day-to-day living, but at any time during the day or night he could focus his mind on the spot in his chest just to reassure himself that it still existed.

Daily meditations were not his style and after a few weeks of bliss he stopped performing the practice on a regular basis. Whenever he felt himself drift sufficiently off course he would play the recordings on his laptop and assume a meditative position until he returned to peace inside.

He felt peace overtake him as he sat on the white plastic chair outside his trailer. He opened his eyes. The sun shone brightly on the green branches of the palo verde trees surrounding the area he had cleared for building his straw-bale home.

He began repeating his mantra as Carol's voice continued. "Ahh-ooo-mmm, ahh-ooo-mmm," he repeated over and over with his deepest and most resonant voice. The vibrations in his vocal chords permeated his jawbone and sinus cavities tickling his nose. He felt the warm spot under his heart returning.

Johnny fixed himself a tall glass of iced tea, heavy on the ice, and then sat back down on the plastic chair in the shade of his trailer. The air was warm. He leaned his head back on the chair and listened to the sounds of the desert. He heard the sound of the windmill rudder creaking as a slight breeze wafted across his face. The rudder normally silently laid against the back of the mill's fan blades, but a strong enough breeze could cause it to shift so that it stuck out behind the blades like the body of an airplane behind a propeller.

Cactus wrens chattered in the palo verde trees in the surrounding desert. For a few hours, Johnny felt at peace staring at the rocky outcropping on the west side of The Huerfano in front of him. He retrieved a cylindrical-shaped mahogany colored wooden flute from his trailer. The traditional Native American musical instrument had a small mouth pieces opening at one end, six finger-holes on top, and a larger opening at the other end where the music escaped.

He received the flute as a gift from Mike Gerrity, the State Police Officer who had comforted him at the time of his wife's death. He had used the flute to pour out his emotions when he had trouble verbalizing them. Although, he had occasionally listened to some Native American flute music, he never tried to learn a specific song. He just let the music come out of him, which he understood to be how some Native Americans used the flute.

He had read that Native American sometimes played the flute as a form of meditation. The flute was said to evoke a feeling one might have when out on a calming mountain or ocean retreat. In Johnny's judgment the hollow wooden instrument fulfilled its promise every time he played. He started playing long slow notes. The notes came to him naturally without any thought. He could feel the release of pressure from his mind and body.

After twenty minutes of playing, Johnny walked over to the makeshift shower near the front of his trailer, stripped naked and then washed himself in the warm morning air. He felt good. His body and mind felt like they were working at their maximum performance level. He dried himself off and put on his shorts and T-shirt. He thought about the advice everyone had given him to take some time for himself. He made up his mind to start building his straw bale house to keep his mind off the events of the week.

As he walked back to his trailer, he stuck his hand into his shorts' pocket and felt a small piece of paper inside. He pulled out the paper and found the note that had been taped to his gate the night before. He perused the handwritten note and the business card attached to the tape. The note indicated that Red Ruby Real Estate was interested in buying his property. It requested that Johnny call the number on the card to discuss an offer with Ruby's lead salesman Bob O'Rielly.

He called the number on the business card attached to the note left on his gate. After several minutes of explaining who he was and why he called and then several more minutes listening to Muzak while on hold, Bob O'Rielly came on the line.

"Mr. Blue, I am glad you called," O'Rielly said. "We are very interested in purchasing your ten acres out on Park Link and would like to sit down with you to talk about an offer."

"Isn't ten acres kind of small for a big developer like Red Ruby?" Johnny asked. "You know it is surrounded by State Trust Land don't you? It's not like you can put up two thousand houses like you did when you bought all those cotton fields in Marana."

"Why don't you just come down to our offices and see what we have to say," O'Rielly said. "We might make you an offer you can't refuse."

"I'll listen with a skeptical ear," Johnny said. "I can make it tomorrow around noon if that's good for you." He finalized the arrangements for the meeting and pressed the disconnect button on his cell phone.

He had a few hours before he had to leave for his tennis match with Jim Morrison. He turned his thoughts to the bales of straw sitting under the blue tarp next to the cement foundation he had laid down the week before. The foundation was ready to accept the walls of straw. He would have liked to have gotten up early and started building the walls of his house before the sun rose too far up in the sky. Since he had slept in, he decided to lay out some of the bales and then build them in the cool evening after his tennis match with Jim Morrison.

He moved towards the bales and began removing the blue tarp that protected them from the environment. The tarp was used to keep the bales dry to prevent them from rotting once they were installed as the walls of his house. He removed the tarp from the bales and spread it out in the sun near the foundation.

The process he planned to follow was to set the bales out in the sun during the day to reduce any moisture hidden inside them and then to start building the walls on a night when he felt energetic. The monsoon on Monday and his aching head on Tuesday prevented him from making that effort earlier in the week. It was now Wednesday; he decided he would try to put up at least one row of bales after his tennis match in the evening.

He planned to build a small structure just big enough for his basic needs. He thought that nine hundred square feet of living space would be sufficient. He had designed the house to form a rectangle with an inside length of forty five feet and an inside width of twenty feet. The straw bales were two feet wide, so he had laid the cement foundation down with four extra feet on each side. Since the bales were three feet long, he knew he needed approximately seventeen bales for the long sides and seven bales for the short sides. This meant that each row of straw bales would contain approximately fifty bales.

He planned to build the walls four rows high. He had around two hundred bales waiting to be laid down, but he would only lay one hundred of them out in the sun. He thought that he would be lucky to put up the first two rows of bales in an eight hour work period after his tennis match. He knew that he would have to build the walls in stages and hope that Mother Nature held off the rains long enough for him to be successful.

Johnny had decided to use straw-bales to build his home because of their desirable qualities as a building material and because the alternative construction material would set his house apart from the boon of wood-framed stucco houses the tract housing developers populated the land with. To Johnny, the desirable qualities of a straw-bale house included super-insulated walls, simple construction, and low cost. He hoped that once he finished construction, he would have a low-cost, elegant, and energy-efficient living space for himself.

He knew that straw-bale construction performed better in the area of fire safety than conventional building materials. According to a report he had read, the straw bales held enough air to provide good insulation value, but because they were compacted firmly, they did not hold enough air to permit combustion. They were virtually fireproof.

The report he read also emphasized the importance of safeguarding the bales against rotting. The most important safeguard was to buy dry bales and keep them dry. He hoped that by laying the bales out in the hot sun all day they would remain dry until he could safely seal them into the walls of the house.

A lot of the plans for the construction of the house were designed to keep the bales dry to prevent rot. The foundation was over six inches above the ground, special plastic would be put between the bales and the foundation, and special interior and exterior paint would be used to prevent moisture from getting trapped into the walls. If the monsoon rains would hold off for another week, Johnny knew that he would have a solid house to last many years.

It took him half an hour to lay out into the sun the one hundred bales he needed for the first two rows for the structure's walls. He sat down on the plastic chair in the shade of his abode. He leaned his head back and stared at the silhouette of the metal windmill against the clear blue sky on the horizon.

CHAPTER 13

At 5:30 P.M. on Wednesday Johnny Blue checked to make sure his tennis racket was still behind the seat in his pickup and then drove down his sandy driveway. Out of the shade of his private hideaway, the hot sun beat down on his red pickup truck. He turned on the air conditioner not wanting to show up at the tennis club drenched in sweat or dehydrated.

He had not been to the club since before he started his job as a part-time security guard for the Faithful Security Agency. After his wife and son died, he used tennis as a way to take his mind off his grief. Over the previous three years he had signed up for one or two six-week group lessons per year as a way to get out of the house.

He had met Jim Morrison at one of the group lessons at the club and they had played together occasionally. Jim played tennis three nights a week and twice on the weekends if he could find enough partners. Johnny and Jim played on Wednesday nights and sometimes on Sunday mornings for a while. When Johnny moved out of Marana to Park Link Drive he decided to take some time off from the courts. The email Johnny received the previous day was not the first time Jim had asked him to fill in for a partner that had to opt out of a match. It was the first time Johnny accepted.

Johnny pulled into the parking lot of the Marana Tennis Club on Tangerine Road. The club was built during Marana's great population boom during the nineteen nineties in anticipation of the future housing developments which soon sprung up in the area along the two lane rural road. Johnny parked his car in front of the two-story building painted saguaro green. He recognized Jim Morrison's black sports car parked next to him. The personalized license plates on the vehicle read "TENSNE1."

Johnny entered the clubhouse through the double glass doors at the entrance, identified himself to the young Hispanic female behind the reception desk, and watched her sign him in on her computer screen. He walked through the lobby and out into the sunshine. A dozen outdoor tennis courts came into view as he stepped outside.

"Over here," Jim Morrison yelled from the third court over.

Johnny jogged over to the court and shook Jim's hand.

"Well look at you," Johnny said. "You look like you've lost a lot of weight."

"Yeah, I've been on a diet," Jim said.

"What kind of diet?" Johnny asked as the two walked to opposite sides of the court and began volleying the ball back and forth across the net. "I need to lose a few pounds myself."

"Lots of tennis, eat in moderation, and take a couple of blue pills every day," Jim replied.

The two began their game. Despite his height and weight disadvantage Johnny's quick reactions and ability to cover the entire court usually surprised his opponents. Morrison was no exception.

"I see you haven't lost a step," Morrison said as he prepared to serve for the win in the tiebreaker session. Morrison slammed the overhead serve past Johnny as if he was standing still.

"Nice shot," Johnny said. "Do you have a cannon over there or what?"

"I had to reach back a little for that one," Morrison said. "We've got time for another match if you want."

Johnny agreed to play again after a short rest. He sat down on the bench between the courts and sipped water from his squeeze bottle. Morrison excused himself to use the restroom. From his vantage point Johnny could see inside Morrison's open bag. Laying on top of a white towel in the bag was a can of tennis balls, two bananas, and two small white bottles.

Johnny read the label on one of the bottles. The writing indicated that the bottle contained a vitamin and mineral supplement. The label on the other bottle was turned face down so Johnny could not read it.

"Ready to play partner?" Morrison said.

Johnny noticed that Morrison was barely sweating while Johnny's own shirt was soaked through with sweat. Johnny wiped the perspiration from his forehead with a towel and took his place on the court.

"Tell me more about this diet," Johnny said. "Does it include eating a lot of bananas?"

"What makes you think that?" Morrison said.

"I just noticed a couple of bananas on top of your bag over there," Johnny replied. "Hope you don't mind."

"Oh that, the pills I take deplete the potassium in my body so I eat bananas," Morrison replied. He served the ball and Johnny made a futile attempt to return it.

"Sounds like a diuretic," Johnny said. Morrison served the ball past him again.

"How about a little more play and a little less talk?" Morrison said.

Each player easily held their serve for twelve games making the score six games each and forcing the tiebreaker again.

"Mind if I take a water break?" Johnny asked. "You can see I'm losing a lot more water than you. I wouldn't want to become dehydrated and die of heat stroke out here."

Morrison frowned and said, "Okay. Not too long though."

"Was Larry Dvorak your old playing partner?" Johnny asked as he sat down on the bench and sipped water from his squeeze bottle. He wiped the sweat from his face with a towel.

"Yes, he was," Morrison said. "How did you know that?"

"You mentioned your playing partner was moving back to Iowa and I knew that Larry was moving there, so I just put two and two together," Johnny said.

"How well did you know him?" Johnny asked.

Morrison zipped up his sports bag and drank from his squeeze bottle while leaning against the pole that held up the net. "We just played tennis on Wednesdays for the last two months," Morrison said. "We didn't talk about anything much except tennis."

"You heard he died up on Picacho didn't you?" Johnny asked.

"I read that in the paper yesterday. I was shocked," Morrison said.

"Did you ever meet his wife?" Johnny asked. "Did she ever come watch him play?"

"I think she did come out once," Jim said. "The first time we played I think."

"She was a little cutie wasn't she," Johnny said.

"I don't recall," Jim said. He pushed himself off of the pole and then walked a circle around the bench Johnny sat on. "Are you ready to play?"

"Sure," Johnny said and stood up off the bench. "When did you see him last?"

"I don't know? I think we stopped playing two weeks ago," Morrison said as he took his place on the court. With his left hand, he rhythmically bounced a tennis ball on the base line. "Can we play?"

"Sorry," Johnny said. "I am just curious about the guy. I am the one that found him out in the desert."

Morrison bounced the ball off of his shoe and it took off across the court and into the net. He walked towards the net to retrieve the ball.

"I did not know that," Morrison said. "Did he say anything when you found him?"

Johnny thought of several questions he would ask someone who had found a dead body. The question Morrison asked was not in Johnny's top ten list.

"Dead men tell no tales," Johnny said. He served the ball past Morrison. Morrison made a feeble swing towards the ball with his racket and missed.

"I guess you shouldn't have let me have that break," Johnny said after winning every point in the tie breaker. He wiped his forehead with his towel. "I am going to head home to take a shower."

"I think I'll take one here," Morrison said.

The two opponents shook hands and complemented each other on their respective games.

On his way out of the reception area Johnny waited to make sure Morrison entered the locker room and then approached the receptionist. The girl behind the desk looked like she was in her late teens. She had a dark complexion and a bright smile. She looked bored as she read from a large textbook on her desk.

"How are you doing tonight?" Johnny said with a smile. "Looks pretty slow."

"I like it that way," the girl responded. "It gives me a chance to do my homework."

"What kind of soda do you like?" Johnny asked as he approached the soda vending machine near the entrance.

"I'm fine with my Diet Coke here," she replied. Johnny purchased a non-carbonated sports drink and walked back to the desk.

"I hate to do this," Johnny said quietly as he leaned over the counter to talk to the girl. "But I think this guy might be fooling around with my wife." The girl let out a gasp.

"Could you tell me if anyone had reservations for six P.M. last Wednesday?" Johnny asked.

"Okay, just a second," the girl whispered. She looked nervously around the room.

"Morrison and Dvorak," she said.

"Did they actually play or just reserve the court," Johnny asked.

"They played," the girl said. "They are both members here and the computer debited one of the fifteen monthly plays they are allowed. In fact I was here last Wednesday and I remember them coming in. They did not play too long. Dvorak left early. He seemed a little upset."

"Any idea why?" Johnny asked.

"He didn't say. He just kind of stormed out of the place," the girl replied. "Hey I thought this was about your wife."

"Oh it is, but I like gossip too," Johnny said. "What about Sunday morning? Did Morrison play his usual set at ten o'clock?"

"It looks like he checked in around ten fifteen," the girl said. "Larry Dvorak's name was on the reservation also, but he never checked in. Morrison checked out a serving machine. Looks like he practiced by himself."

"Thanks," Johnny said. "I'd appreciate it if we could keep this our little secret. Let me contribute something to your college fund." Johnny dropped a twenty dollar bill over the counter on to the girl's open textbook. She stealthily grabbed the bill and slipped it in between the pages in her book.

Johnny walked out into the warm night air as the sun was setting in the west. The western horizon lit up with every shade of orange and purple.

He drove down the interstate towards Park Link Drive. He thought about the match with Morrison. He seemed a little nervous, especially around the subject of the Dvorak's deaths and diuretics. Morrison said that he only played with Dvorak on Wednesdays, but Dvorak's name was on the reservation for Sunday also even though he never showed up. He wondered why Morrison would lie about the Sunday match and why he had not contacted Johnny to play on Sunday as well as Wednesday if Dvorak was not going to be there.

Johnny wondered if Morrison was really using a diuretic as some kind of weight loss method. He could not tell what was in the second bottle in Morrison's bag. If Morrison was using a diuretic for weight loss, it did not make any sense to Johnny. The effect of the diuretic would be to lose water weight only. Morrison would gain any weight back as soon as he drank more water unless he continued to take the pills on a daily basis. That would be dangerous to his health.

When Johnny reached his trailer, he was exhausted from the physical activity and the loss of fluids from his body. He saw the bales of straw laid out in the fading sunlight and knew his day had just begun.

CHAPTER 14

Johnny examined the layout of the cement foundation after arriving home from his tennis match with Jim Morrison. Pieces of rebar one-half inch in diameter stuck up four feet above the concrete surface. The metal bars were equally spaced every two feet around the fifty foot by twenty one foot rectangular foundation.

He filled a large glass with iced tea, donned his work gloves, and approached the cement foundation. He started his work by carefully laying down asphalt paper around the edge of the foundation so that the straw bale walls would have protection from moisture from underneath. As he centered the paper over the rebar he punched a hole in it to allow it to slide down the cross-hatched metal posts. He carefully adjusted the paper into position and then started building the walls with the bales of straw one bale at a time.

The sun began to set in the west as the moon began to rise in the east. The moon was nearly half full and would provide ample light for the remaining work.

The first row of bales would take the most time to setup since he had to ensure the bales were lined up exactly as they should be with each other and with the foundation. He methodically grabbed one bale, positioned it over the rebar and pressed it down until it set flat on the foundation. He used a straight edge to ensure that the bale was positioned within a small tolerance. He repeated the process one bale at a time as he proceeded around the perimeter of the cement foundation. After the first row of bales was in place, he stepped back to take a look at his work. He sipped iced tea from a tall glass as a feeling of accomplishment grew inside him.

He wiped the sweat from his brow and sat down on one of the plastic patio chairs near his trailer. He knew that any exertion in the dry heat of the Sonoran Desert sucked the energy out of a person. It took him nearly four hours to put down the first row of bales. He could feel his energy draining away.

He got up out of the plastic chair, put on his work gloves and began putting up the second row of straw bales. He methodically positioned the bales one at a time over the rebar and pushed them down into place over the first row.

Putting up the second row of bales took over two hours to accomplish. He could see the outline of his home taking shape as he stood back to admire the four foot tall structure.

He had kept the design simple leaving a wide space for double doors on the back and smaller spaces for single doors on the other sides of the structure. He left a wide opening in the second row of bales for a large window facing Picacho Peak from what he intended to be his living room. The other windows for the structure would begin to take shape as he put up the subsequent rows of straw bales. Once he had all the rows of bales up, he would need to pin them by pounding lengths of rebar from the top to the bottom. Only then would he be able to add the wooden frames for the windows and doors.

He refilled his glass with iced tea and sat down on the white plastic chair in front of his trailer. He felt exhausted and dehydrated. He had worked for six hours in the moonlight in temperatures reaching the low-nineties. He imagined how weak and dehydrated the Dvoraks must have felt on their four hour odyssey on Picacho Peak in one hundred seven degree heat in bright sunshine. Maybe it was just a case of ignorance and stupidity that caused their deaths, he thought.

He thought about his tennis match with Jim Morrison. Morrison's actions seemed a little suspicious to him, but that did not mean he had anything to do with the death of the Dvoraks. He tried to think of a motive for Morrison.

He did not know Morrison that well and knew even less about his relationship with the Dvoraks. Morrison seemed like one of those wheeler-dealer types always trying to sell something but not very good at it. Maybe he got the Dvorak's mixed up in a scam and they lost some money over it. Maybe that was why Larry Dvorak left the club so upset the week before. But then why kill them? Johnny thought. They were leaving town. Maybe they threatened to sue or go to the police.

Johnny finished the night by covering the entire structure with black plastic and throwing the blue tarp back over the rest of the bales under the ramada next to his trailer. He hoped to continue the routine the next day by laying out more bales to dry in the sun during the day to be put up on the structure in the evening.

He sat down inside his trailer and turned on the fan at the rear. The fan rattled the walls of the trailer as the cool air blew in from the open window in the back through the trailer to the open window in the front. He could hear the sound of the windmill rudder creaking as a light breeze blew outside.

He tried to recall his impression of Morrison's personality. Morrison was the kind of guy that bragged about his sexual conquests. Johnny always took his descriptions of liaisons with both single and married women with a grain of salt. When Johnny used to play with him on a regular basis, he was much heavier and it was hard to believe that his physical attributes would attract such a wide variety of women. Johnny thought that Morrison's personality came off as arrogant and snobbish to most people. He saw Morrison strike out a few times with women in the tennis class and he was not a pleasant person to be around afterwards. Was this the personality of a murderer, he wondered.

Johnny laid down on his bed in his trailer and drifted off to sleep with the image of Josephine Dvorak's parched face in his mind.

CHAPTER 15

Johnny Blue spent Thursday morning removing the blue tarp from the straw bales stacked under the ramada next to his trailer. He had slept in again so the summer sun was already high in the sky when he began to lay out the bales of straw to be used as the next layer on the walls of his house.

He spread the tarp out in the sun and laid approximately one hundred bales on top of it in a single layer. He thought that if he could put up one hundred more bales in the evening, he would be very close to having the walls of his house ready for inspection. All that he would have left to do would be to pin the straw bale walls from top to bottom using eight foot lengths of rebar. He would save that final task for another day.

After a quick shower, he changed into a fresh set of shorts and a long-sleeved T-shirt for his meeting with Bob O'Rielly of Red Ruby Real Estate. He had a preconceived notion of how the meeting would go and tried to prepare himself. His focus for the last several months was to put himself in a position where he could live a simple life of solitude in the desert. Now that his goal was within his grasp, he did not want to give up on it by selling out to a large development corporation. He would listen to any offer O'Rielly made, but it would take a lot for him to give up his land. Mainly he wanted to find out what plans the developer had for the area so he could stay one step ahead of him.

The morning air was warm as Johnny drove to the Marana office of Red Ruby Real Estate five miles from the old town area on Tangerine Road. He pulled into the parking lot of the strip mall lined with off-white stucco buildings with large shiny gold letters identifying upscale real estate and law offices. He parked in front of the Red Ruby Real Estate office and stepped out of his car into the bright sunlight.

The receptionist's greeting was cold and short. Johnny suspected his outfit of a wrinkled T-shirt, shorts and sandals tipped her off that he was not a prospective purchaser of one of their top properties. Johnny informed her of his appointment to see Bob O'Rielly. She turned away from him as she spoke into the telephone receiver.

"Mr. O'Rielly will be right with you," the receptionist said. "Why don't you have a seat?"

Johnny sat down on the firm charcoal gray leather couch facing the receptionist's desk. He perused a catalog of hot properties in the area and wondered what it must be like to desire such opulence. He recalled selling his house in the Tortolita Mountains a few miles away for $150,000 two months earlier. There was not a house in the catalog priced at less than five times that amount.

A tall man in his thirties wearing an expensive suit walked out of an office behind the receptionist's desk. He was followed by a thin woman in her late twenties talking animatedly with her hands. She wore an immaculately clean and pressed gold blazer and short white skirt. Her long golden hair bounced around her shoulders as she talked.

"I really think we can get these guys to commit if we can fly them down here in mid-October when the weather starts to cool off," Johnny overheard her say.

"All right set it up and put it on my schedule so I can take them out on the course when they are here," the man said in a deep calm voice. "I'll be at the club the rest of the afternoon."

Another woman with long blond hair arrived in the lobby from the carpeted stairs on the other end of the room. "Mr. Blue?" the woman said as she approached Johnny.

"Yes," Johnny replied. He jumped to his feet as if he was startled from his sleep.

"Mr. O'Rielly will see you now," the woman said. "Follow me please."

Johnny followed her up the stairs and sensed that she and the receptionist were both aware that he was eyeing her legs. She showed him to a large corner office on the second floor overlooking the flat non-descript area known as Avra Valley. Cotton fields still made up a majority of the land in the valley, but a noticeable dent in the flat bare landscape had been made by recent tract housing developments being developed by Red Ruby Real Estate.

Bob O'Rielly held out his hand and Johnny shook it firmly. O'Rielly was of medium height and medium build wearing the eyeglasses of an accountant on his balding head. His smile was broad and sincere. Johnny guessed that the man must have closed a lot of deals with that smile.

O'Rielly asked Johnny to sit in one of two leather chairs in front of his desk. Johnny wrapped his bare legs around the wooden legs of the chair and grasped the leather arms tightly as if he was about to take off on a roller coaster ride.

"How do you like that place out on Park Link Drive?" O'Rielly asked. "I hear you want to put up a straw-bale house out there. That type of construction seems to be pretty popular with the independent crowd like yourself."

"I like it," Johnny said. "You said you had an offer for me?"

"All business, aren't you?" O'Rielly said. "All right, we can get down to business if you like. We want to offer you twice what you paid for the land two months ago. That's cash, free and clear you can do what you want with the money."

"What do you want with my little piece of property?" Johnny asked.

"Good question," O'Rielly said. "There is no secret that it is a great little piece of property you have there. It's secluded and you have views of every mountain range around. We have a prospective client that is looking for something similar to your place and is willing to pay top dollar for it."

"That place was on the market for several years before I bought it a few months ago," Johnny said. "Why all the sudden interest?"

"This client of ours is from out of town. He recently contacted us and told us what he was looking for. We searched our database and came up with your land," O'Rielly said.

"I am not buying it," Johnny said. "Except for the tract housing you guys sell at a dime a dozen, the kind of clients you guys deal with want a few acres in a resort community in a canyon somewhere like in the Tortolitas. Ten acres in the middle of nowhere won't cut it for the kind of people you deal with."

"This customer is special," O'Rielly said. "We'd like to accommodate them as well as you. We'd like to make this a win-win situation.

"I'll tell you what; I've got a line on some acreage over on the east side of the Tortolitas that might be just right for you. If you play ball with us I'll see what I can do about getting you into something over there. You won't have the view of Picacho Peak, but you'll be in the Tortolitas and not far from the Catalinas."

"I don't like that area," Johnny said. "I like the property I have. Aren't you trying to run the farmers out on the south side of the interstate and develop over there?"

"I can't comment on any deals we have pending," O'Rielly replied. "But we are not trying to run anyone out of anywhere. We are all win-win around here."

"I was just wondering if maybe you decided you could not get the land on the south side from the farmers so you were trying your hand at getting the land on the north side instead," Johnny replied. "The north side would be more suitable for the kind of golf resorts you guys like to put up since it has more mountains and canyons."

"You said yourself we can't touch the land around your acreage because it is State Trust Land," O'Rielly replied. "This is a one shot deal."

"You would know better than I whether there is some kind of loophole around that problem," Johnny said. "Didn't you guys swap some farmland you bought so you could build on State Trust Land in the Tortolitas?"

"I'll tell you what," O'Rielly said as he stood up and walked around his desk. "Why don't you think about it over the weekend and let me know your answer on Monday." He shook Johnny's hand and led him to his office door. "Mary will show you the way out."

Johnny drove to the Marana Library and parked in the nearly empty parking lot. He greeted Joanne Masters and put his name down to use one of the two library computers. "Have you heard anything about any new developments Red Ruby has in mind around here?" Johnny asked.

"I know he has been trying to buy up some of those cotton fields near Red Rock," Joanne said. "They say he wants to put up a resort out there, but that land is so flat I don't see how they could."

"How could I find out what kind of land purchases he has made in the area recently?" Johnny asked.

"You could go to the Pima and Pinal County assessor web page and search by their name and date," she replied. "They have a couple of other company names they use also but they always use Ruby in the name."

After pointing Johnny to the right web page on the computer, the librarian pulled up a chair beside him. "What is this all about?" she asked.

"Probably nothing," Johnny said as he typed in the search information on the assessor's web site. "They just offered me twice what I paid for my land a few months ago. They said some out of town buyer wants it. I'd like to know what they are up to."

"No good. I am sure of that," the librarian replied.

A list of two dozen properties purchased in the previous year by any entity with the word "Ruby" in their name came up on the computer screen. "Except for one property near Picacho Peak, it looks like he has been busy purchasing property along Park Link," Johnny said. "How can I plot these properties on a map?"

"Open up another browser and go to the Pima and Pinal Geographical Information System web site," she said. "Search for Ruby's name again and it will let you see a map of his holdings. Then you can zoom into Park Link Drive."

Johnny did as instructed and soon had a GIS map showing all the major geographical features around Park Link Drive. State Trust Land was colored a solid light gray. Property owned by anyone named Ruby had red cross-hatches over it. Other private land had blue diagonal lines.

"How much to print this out?" Johnny asked.

"Fifty cents a page," the librarian answered. "Did you find what you are looking for?"

"Maybe," Johnny said. He waited for the two page map to print and then handed Joanne a dollar bill. "I am going to go home and get some rest. I have to be back at work tomorrow," he said.

CHAPTER 16

As he traveled northwest on Interstate 10 Johnny thought about the offer O'Rielly had made for his property. There was something fishy about it, but he did not know what. He wondered why that even concerned him. It was a good deal for him if he would take it.

He was already starting to sour on the idea of building his straw-bale house. After the events of the last few days he wondered if it was possible for him or anyone else to hide from the world anymore. If it was not possible, he wondered how he should deal with it. Maybe he could take the money Ruby was offering and travel the United States in his pickup truck and trailer. He could stay at different campgrounds for weeks at a time like a normal retired person.

He drove up fast on the back of a black nineteen eighties model Ford pickup traveling well below the seventy five miles per hour speed limit. The pickup had a black canopy on the back and the tailgate had multiple rusty dents. As Johnny slowed his vehicle and waited for the passing lane to clear, the left rear wheel of the black pickup suddenly shot out across the interstate to the median.

The left side of the pickup's rear end sunk to the pavement and the front end veered to the right. The truck violently rolled over three times as it crashed through the ditch and fences lining the interstate. A body flew out of the passenger's side of the cab of the pickup as Johnny passed by in his own vehicle.

Johnny turned on his flashers and slowed to a stop a few hundred yards past the demolished black pickup. The truck lay on its side in the ditch and Johnny could see people crawling painfully out of the back. He dialed nine one one on his cell phone, informed the dispatcher of the accident and then walked towards the wreck to offer assistance.

Already several other cars had stopped near the wreck and traffic began to backup on the interstate. Two men lay on their backs about fifteen feet in front of the pickup. Johnny could hear them groaning in pain as he approached. A gray haired man tried to calm the two. At least twenty males and females of Mexican heritage lined the fence beside the ditch. Some of the shaken and injured people sat down in the dirt along the fence.

Johnny knew the scene well from descriptions of similar accidents in the newspapers. A *coyote* or illegal alien smuggler must have been transporting his cargo up to Phoenix for dispersing around the country for illegal work. The *coyote*s were known to use throwaway vehicles on their last legs and often crashed violently on the interstate while making their runs. The description of the carnage from such wrecks made Johnny even more sympathetic to the plight of the border crossers. Now he was witnessing the carnage first hand.

A blue Ford pickup with a canopy similar to the wrecked vehicle pulled up next to the accident. The canopy door opened and the illegals standing in the ditch rushed over. A dozen or more climbed inside the packed vehicle before the canopy door shut again. The blue pickup drove away on the pavement alongside the freeway. It passed by the interstate travelers who had slowed to gawk at the accident. Johnny wrote down the license plate of the vehicle as it passed by him.

He could hear the sounds of sirens approaching. The illegals that could move climbed the fence and scattered into the desert to the northeast of the freeway.

"I am a nurse," one lady said as she approached the scene from her car parked a hundred yards away. She started directing others to help calm the victims or hold their heads to keep them from moving in case there were any spinal injuries.

Deputy Sheriff Juan Dugas was the first official person to arrive at the scene. He recognized Johnny immediately and approached him after making a quick survey of the situation and after an ambulance arrived and two State Police officers took charge of the accident scene.

"You just can't seem to stay out of trouble can you?" he said.

"Must be my lucky week," Johnny said. "I was right behind them when their rear wheel came off and they flipped over. Looks like another *coyote* too cheap to buy decent transportation for his cargo."

"Looks that way," the deputy said as he wrote down the information in his notebook.

"Another one pulled up after the accident and picked up about half the survivors," Johnny said. "The other half scattered in the desert. I got the license and description of the other vehicle if you want it. You might be able to have them picked up before they get to Phoenix in the next hour."

Johnny gave the deputy the information and the deputy wrote it down in his notebook.

"I thought you were going to stay home and get some rest," the deputy said.

"Have you heard anything yet on the autopsy on that couple that died on Picacho Peak?" Johnny asked.

"Simple case of heat stroke," the deputy answered. "Case closed."

As he spoke the words, a single gunshot rang out from the desert on the other side of the knoll between the freeway and Frontage Road. The deputy drew his gun and both he and Johnny ran to the top of the knoll covered with tall brown dried grass.

Johnny recognized the green camouflage painted Bronco parked on Frontage Road across from the accident on the freeway. A tall man wearing a camouflage hunting outfit stood near the front of the vehicle. He cradled an automatic rifle on the hood of the Bronco and pointed it towards the creosote covered desert landscape lining Frontage Road. Three other men dressed in camouflage outfits pointed their rifles at a group of half a dozen illegals a few yards in front of the vehicle.

"Put the gun down," the deputy yelled at the man near the front of the Bronco. He held his revolver in both hands and pointed it at the man. "Put it down."

The man slowly turned towards the deputy then set the butt of the rifle on the ground and leaned the barrel against the side of the front fender. He leaned against the fender and folded his arms across his chest facing the deputy.

"Step to the rear of the vehicle," the deputy said. The man moved to the back of the vehicle and resumed his position with folded arms.

The deputy turned towards the men pointing their guns at the illegals. "All of you put your guns down," the deputy said.

"Hey these guys are gonna run," one of the men yelled back.

"Put your guns down on the ground now," the deputy screamed back. "Put your guns down and walk backwards towards your vehicle."

The men put their rifles down on the ground and slowly backed away from the group of Hispanic men and women. The illegals stayed where they were. A large white Ford Explorer with blue flashing lights on top and a wide green stripe painted down the side with the words "Border Patrol" painted in gold quickly pulled up alongside the group of border crossers. Two uniformed officers jumped out of the vehicle and surrounded the group.

With his gun still drawn, the deputy walked towards the men near the Bronco As he walked down the side of the knoll towards the Bronco he yelled at the men not to move. Officer Mike Gerrity pulled up along the interstate with the lights flashing on his State Police vehicle. He got out of the car, drew his gun and rushed to Deputy Dugas' side.

"You hold the three at the front of the vehicle. I'll take care of the guy in the rear," the deputy said.

Officer Gerrity ordered the three men to put their hands on the hood of the Bronco and they obliged. Deputy Dugas ordered the man at the back of the vehicle to turn around, put his hands on his head and spread his legs. The man obliged. The deputy handcuffed the man and searched him. He retrieved a large hunting knife from the man's boot and set it on the ground near the vehicle.

"You better hope you didn't hit anyone," Johnny heard the deputy yell in the man's ear. "Did you?"

The man shook his head no. Johnny sat down in the dry grass and watched as the two police officers took the men into custody and the Border Patrol officers rounded up the illegal border crossers. As other law enforcement personnel arrived they scoured the desert for more illegals and a possible shooting victim. Two more ambulances arrived and began treating the victims.

Johnny waited for half an hour before he could get the deputy's attention and ask permission to leave. The deputy asked him to fill out another witness form with information about everything he saw. As he filled out the form, a small bright yellow helicopter landed nearby on the road. Two of the accident victims were loaded into the helicopter and flown away.

Johnny felt compassion for the victims, but he wondered how many thousands of dollars of American taxpayer's money would be spent to treat the people that had never paid a dime of American taxes in their lives. He understood their plight, but as with most injustices in the world the wrong people seemed to have to pay the price for the misdeeds of others.

Johnny handed the witness form to the deputy. The deputy took the form and thanked him for sticking around.

"I just hope you can find some peace and quiet on that ranch of yours," the deputy said as Johnny walked back to his pickup. Johnny started his vehicle and drove down the interstate towards Park Link Drive.

CHAPTER 17

Johnny Blue drove his red pickup northwest along the interstate away from the scene of the automobile accident, exited on to Park Link Drive and then drove down the dirt road to the travel trailer on his desert ranch. He saw the straw bales laid out in the fading sunlight and knew he still had work to do before he retired for the night. He filled a large glass with iced tea, donned his work gloves, and approached the cement foundation.

He started grabbing bales from where they lay in the fading sun on the blue tarp near the foundation for his house. He methodically positioned the straw on top of the two rows of bales he had laid down the night before. The bottom two rows completely covered the rebar sticking up from the foundation. Johnny tightly packed the third row in place without the use of rebar to hold them. Once he had the third and fourth rows in place he would pin the top two rows to the bottom two with rebar. It took him two hours to put up the third row of bales.

The wall was now six feet tall and above his head. The fourth row would be much more difficult to put up. He would have to throw a bale over his head on top of the third row and then use a ladder to help him position it precisely in place.

He laid out the fourth row of bales inside the four walls of his house and then set a sturdy aluminum step ladder in place. He threw the first bale over his head and laid it on top of the third row of bales, climbed up the ladder, positioned the bale in place, climbed down the ladder, and then moved the ladder three feet further along the wall. He picked up the next bale, threw it over his head on to the third row next to the bale he had just positioned in place. He climbed back up the ladder and positioned the bale into place. He repeated the process for all the bales on the fourth row. After three hours, he had an eight foot high wall of straw bales that formed the enclosure for his house.

He wiped the sweat from his brow and brushed pieces of straw off of his sweat soaked T-shirt. Johnny sat down on the plastic chair in front of his trailer and brushed the straw out of his hair. He sipped on his refilled glass of iced tea and tried to catch his breath. The dry air was draining away his energy.

He thought about what the sheriff said about finding peace on his ranch. After the exertion of putting up the final rows of straw bales, he felt at peace but wondered how long it would last. He wondered if his theory of the journey being more important than the destination would come back to haunt him. It was as if he had no destination in mind for whatever journey lay ahead of him for the rest of his life. Nietzsche once wrote something about how forgetting the goal of a journey was the most frequent stupidity in which people indulged themselves. Johnny tried to remember what the goal of his journey was without feeling stupid.

He enjoyed building his house out in the solitude of the desert, but what would become of him once the structure was complete and he had reached his destination. Would he become bored with life and look for another journey to pursue?

That is where his travel trailer came in, he thought. There were some things he would like to do around the ranch such as writing short stories or possibly even a novel or maybe even raising cattle. But if he ever got bored he could always hook up the trailer to his pickup and head out for parts unknown. He could become the happy wanderer and still have a fortress of solitude in the desert to return to and recount his adventures to himself.

It sounded like a pipe dream; like something that even if achieved would leave him empty inside. How long could he stand to be alone, he wondered. He knew that if he lived the life he just described to himself that he would grow ever more reclusive with each passing year. He imagined himself ten years in the future with a graying scraggly beard wearing torn and dirty clothes with a torn and dirty hat patrolling his ranch with a shotgun in his hand defending his property from imaginary enemies. He imagined himself with no teeth sipping whiskey from a flask rocking back and forth on a rocking chair on the porch in front of his straw-bale house caressing the shotgun lying on his lap. Was this the life he wanted for himself, he wondered.

He finished the night by covering the entire straw-bale structure with black plastic and throwing the blue tarp back over the rest of the bales under the ramada next to his trailer.

He sat down inside his trailer and turned on the fan at the rear. The fan rattled the walls as the cool air blew in from the open window in the back and then through the open window in the front. He laid down on his bed and fell asleep with the now familiar image of Josephine Dvorak's face staring at him through his closed eyelids.

CHAPTER 18

Johnny awoke to the pleasant sound of cactus wrens chattering and turtle doves cooing outside his trailer on Friday morning. After his morning ablutions he called Tammy Macy, a secretary he knew at Sungod Industries. He told her that he wanted to discuss some gossip and she eagerly agreed to meet with him for lunch at a restaurant in Marana.

He fixed himself a breakfast of scrambled eggs and sausage over a single propane fueled burner in his kitchen. He sat down at the table in his trailer and ravenously ate the breakfast and drank from a tall glass of iced tea.

Johnny spent an hour spreading out enough rebar inside his newly built walls to allow him to pin the walls together from top to bottom using eight foot lengths of metal rod. He would have to use the step ladder to get up high enough to pin the bales so he laid out the rebar to minimize the effort required to locate a metal rod before climbing up the ladder. After he had the rebar laid out the way he wanted it, he returned to his trailer for a refill of a tall glass of iced tea.

During the night he had dreamt of troubleshooting a bug in a piece of software at Sungod. In the dream he was surrounded by his wife Carol and son Jerry along with Josephine and Larry Dvorak. The onlookers were urging him to solve the problem while he sat staring at a blank computer screen. The dream gave him an idea.

He opened up his laptop computer and executed the software troubleshooting program he used to use when he worked at Sungod Industries. The program was designed to allow the user to walk down the events that led up to a problem in any piece of software and to hopefully determine what caused the problem. Johnny wondered if the same program could be used to help him determine what caused the deaths of the couple on the peak. He set up a project in the program to define an event to include *time, date, place, persons involved, activity, cause* and *motive.* He also included a comments field to allow him to make comments on the events.

For the first event he typed in the time the Dvoraks left their house in Marana on Sunday morning. The newspaper said that they left at 10:00 A.M. For the second event he typed in Jim Morrison's arrival at the tennis club at 10:15 A.M. He entered a comment for this event indicating that although he apparently knew Larry Dvorak would not be available to play on Sunday, Morrison only asked Johnny to be his replacement on the following Wednesday, not Sunday. This could mean that Morrison found someone else he intended to play with who did not show up, or he had no intention of playing tennis with anyone on Sunday.

For the third event, Johnny typed in his own check of the State Park area around 10:15 A.M. He noted in a comment that he did not see the Dvorak's vehicle or the crystals at that time. For the fourth event Johnny typed in the Dvorak's arrival at the State Park which he estimated to be around 10:25 A.M. based on the driving distance from Marana and assuming no stops in between. He noted in the comments that they each drank about a quarter of a liter of water before arriving at the park based on the level of water left in the bottles on their console in their car. For the fifth event Johnny put down his own arrival at his trailer at approximately twelve o'clock noon. He noted in his comments that this left Picacho Peak and the surrounding area without a security patrol.

For the sixth event, Johnny also typed in twelve o'clock noon as the time that the couple probably reached the top of the peak. In his comments he indicated that this was an estimate based on an average hike to the top of the peak. He assumed that the couple had made it to the top because Mike Gerrity had told him that the search and rescue team had found evidence of vomit on the other side of the saddle of the peak, which meant that they at least made it over halfway. Johnny also indicated that the time estimate could be higher if the couple were delayed for any reason or slowed down by the heat.

For the seventh event, Johnny typed in 2:00 P.M. as the time of the couple's arrival back at the Hunter Trail trailhead. He made similar comments about the possible inaccuracy of the time due to delays on the trail. The eighth event was the death of the couple which he estimated to be between 2:30 P.M. and 3:00 P.M. based on the assumption that heat stroke does not kill a person instantly but is most likely an excruciatingly painful experience.

Johnny had left the *cause* and *motive* fields blank on the first seven events. For the eighth event, the two deaths, he typed in *unknown* for both fields. If the deaths were simply the result of an errant couple making a fatal mistake, he would later fill in *heatstroke* and *stupidity* in the fields. Unlike Deputy Dugas, Johnny was not convinced the deaths were as simple as they seemed.

For the ninth event, Johnny typed in 3:00 P.M. as the time he started his patrol of the canal near Park Link Drive. In the comments he noted that the Picacho Peak area was under surveillance again. He thought that if any foul play were taking place around the canal, it would have taken place between twelve o'clock noon and 3:00 P.M. the time he was not on patrol. He completed the list with the time he found the bodies and then later found the crystals near the canal.

He looked at the list and knew that he did not have enough information to decide one way or the other. It seemed to him that the couple drank enough water on the drive out to the state park and on the hike to the top of the peak to at least keep them alive for five hours even in the hundred and seven degree heat. However something had caused them to start vomiting on their way back; whether it was the heat, a flu bug or a diuretic, Johnny had no way of knowing. According to Deputy Dugas the autopsy gave no indication of anything other than heat exhaustion.

He thought that the exercise of recording the events was not much help in solving the crime. He recalled that the software was never much help in troubleshooting computer problems at Sungod Industries either. The software helped him organize his thoughts and lead him down the path to a possible solution, but ultimately his subconscious mind would have to spend time processing the information into something coherent before he would get anywhere.

The weakness in the software was that it did not help very much with the cause and effect of the problem. What he needed was another methodology that dealt with why things happened. He remembered from some old detective television show that the key to solving a crime was to define the *method, motive* and *opportunity*.

Assuming that the deaths by dehydration were no accident, the strongest case for *method* had to be that someone slipped something into the couple's water to make them dehydrated. As far as he knew there was no physical evidence of anyone being around at the time of the deaths and forcing them to sit down and die of heatstroke. However, he could not completely discount the idea that someone did not catch them at the end of their hike and force them to die in their weakened state.

There were pin-prick marks on the woman's leg and the man's fingers, but he had dismissed them as the result of an encounter with a cholla or cactus. Was it possible that the marks were needle marks and that someone had injected something in the couple to make them die of dehydration? Johnny did not know enough about injecting anyone with anything to say if it was possible or not. He was getting off-track, he thought. He was starting to sound paranoid; like he was making the case too complicated. The simplest explanation was usually the correct one, he thought.

For *motive* he wondered about his initial findings that the crystals near the canal lined up directly with Wymola Bluff which could possibly provide cover for any activity around the canal. The bluff would not provide cover from anyone looking down from Picacho Peak, however.

Was it possible that the Dvoraks saw some activity related to the crystals near the canal? If so, Johnny wondered if whoever left the crystals near the canal could have known that they were spotted and tried to prevent the Dvoraks from telling anyone. It seemed far fetched owing to the fact that except for the pin-prick marks on the bodies, there was no physical evidence of violence that would cause one to think that someone was actually around when the couple died and somehow physically caused their deaths. However, he did not completely discount the idea that someone accomplished the feat and cleverly covered their tracks.

According to his chemist friend at Sungod, the crystals were some kind of herbicide used to clear land of weeds and shrubs. Why would anyone be clearing weeds in the area between Wymola Bluff and the canal, Johnny wondered. Farmers and land developers would have access to the herbicide. He wondered if the farmers were planning to clear the land and turn it into another cotton field. He also wondered if someone like

Red Ruby had a motive for clearing the land as part of his development activities.

Suddenly Johnny remembered one other event that he neglected to put on his list. CAP refused delivery of water to the farmers on Monday morning. He added that event to his list using the troubleshooting program. Was it possible that whoever had the herbicide had accidentally or purposely leaked it into the canal and set off the CAP's water quality monitor? He made a note that he would need more information about the shutdowns.

Sherry at the Laundromat had said that her son had caught an eco-terrorist trying to poison the farmer's irrigation canal. Could the eco-terrorist have tried the same thing on a larger scale with the CAP canal, he wondered. The idea seemed far fetched since it was his understanding that the amount of water in the canal was so great that any chemical a terrorist might put in the canal would be seriously diluted before it was delivered to any customers.

After the September eleventh terrorist attacks on New York and Washington, D.C., the local newspaper ran several articles on possible terrorist threats in the Tucson area. The newspaper had said that it would take many tankers full of a poison to have any affect on the quality of the drinking water from the CAP canal. Johnny did not remember any mention of how much poison it would take to affect agricultural crops using the same water.

Jack Cecum mentioned that he found a case in New Mexico where an herbicide was washed into the irrigation canals by monsoon rains. But that herbicide was spread from the air. Johnny just assumed that it was distributed in much more massive quantities than anyone on the ground could possibly get out to the canal by land. Would a tanker truck a week be enough to set off the CAP quality alarms or cause cotton fields

to die if the water were used to irrigate the plants?
Johnny did not think so.

Another event crossed his mind and he added it to
the list. The fire at the Indian trading post seemed that
it might be related to the other events. He recalled that
the truck destroyed in the fire had dual rear wheels and
that dual wheeled tracks were found near the crystals
by the canal.

He looked at the map he had printed out at the
library. The one property owned by Red Ruby that was
not located on Park Link Drive was located near
Picacho Peak. The map was not of high enough
resolution for Johnny to tell if the property was the
trading post or not. He would have to use the library to
verify that Red Ruby owned the trading post to possibly
link the real estate developer to the truck. He wondered
if the Sheriff and State Police knew who owned the
property and the truck.

Then there was Jim Morrison. Johnny could fill in
an answer for *opportunity* and *method* for Morrison. He
was late for his Sunday morning tennis match and thus
had *opportunity* to see the couple before they began
their hike. Johnny believed that Morrison had access to
a diuretic as part of his dieting habits. The diuretic
could have been the *method* used to induce dehydration
and heat stroke.

Unfortunately, Johnny could not think of a
reasonable *motive* for Morrison. The Dvoraks were
leaving town the next day and any beef they had with
Morrison, based on the apparent argument Morrison
had with Larry on Wednesday, would seemingly be
resolved when they left.

One more event crossed Johnny's mind and he
added it to the project in the software. The murder of
the illegal aliens near Red Rock was discovered soon
after Johnny found the bodies of the Dvoraks. Was it
possible that the Dvoraks witnessed the crime on their

hike up the peak? If they did, was it possible that they were discovered and whoever killed the illegal aliens somehow killed the Dvoraks to keep them quiet?

He created a new project in his troubleshooting software program and defined fields for *suspect, method, motive* and *opportunity.* He filled in a row with "unknown persons" as a suspect. For method, motive and opportunity he typed "physical restraint," "cover-up of possible illegal activities with crystals near the canal," and "near the peak at the time of the hike" in the respective fields. He wondered if he could be more specific on the identification of the suspects. He added "farmers, developers, or eco-terrorists" to the suspect field.

He added another row to the database with "unknown illegal alien killers" as a suspect. For method, motive and opportunity he typed "physical restraint," "cover-up of possible murders near Red Rock," and "near the peak at the time of the hike" in the respective fields. He adjusted the suspect field by typing in "farmers, militia, alien smugglers."

Finally he added another row with "Jim Morrison" as the suspect. He typed in "diuretic poison," "argument with Dvoraks over unknown subject," and "in Marana before Dvoraks left for hike" for the remaining fields.

Johnny stared at the computer screen. There were still some questions that would need to be answered before a clear suspect emerged. He wrote down the unresolved issues on a notepad. He wrote down that he needed to know what Morrison argued about with Larry Dvorak, who left the crystals in the desert and who killed the illegal aliens near Red Rock. Although he felt that the professionals should handle finding the answers to the latter two, he wondered if there was any information he could gather that would help them.

He stepped outside his trailer with a tall glass of iced tea. He sat down on one of the white plastic patio chairs and began to think about the unknowns in the case. He needed to find out if Jim Morrison had any contact with the Dvoraks on Sunday and what his argument was with Larry. He needed to verify Red Ruby's ownership of the trading post and the dual wheeled truck. He also needed to find out why the CAP water was shutdown on consecutive Mondays. He needed to revisit the library before his evening patrol.

CHAPTER 19

At the Marana Library Johnny verified that Red Ruby Real Estate had purchased the trading post a year earlier. He asked Joanne, the librarian, if she knew anything about CAP refusing delivery of water to the farmers on the previous three Mondays. She said she did not, but she could make a call to the irrigation district for Red Rock to find out if they knew anything.

Johnny stood by her desk and stared across the bookshelves through the tinted windows to the park across the street from the library. He wondered how many people in the Red Rock area would benefit and how many would suffer if Red Ruby bought the farmer's land and put up another Master Planned Community. Joanne hung up the phone.

"Mary Ellen, the secretary for the water department said that the quality alarms went off because the particulate count was too high," Joanne said. "By the time they shut down delivery to the farmers, the particulate count was back to normal.

"They don't know what set off the alarms. They are still analyzing the samples they took. She said that a couple of the farmers were in this morning complaining that their crops were dying. Does that help you?"

"It doesn't help me, but it is interesting gossip isn't it?" Johnny said. "I am sure the professionals know how to handle the situation. I have a lunch date before I go on patrol. Thank you for your help."

"Thank you for making the day so interesting," Joanne replied.

Johnny parked his pickup truck in the parking lot of the restaurant on Orange Grove Road on the eastern edge of the city of Marana. He went inside and found Tammy Macy sitting at a table drinking lemonade.

In her blue polyester pants and pink sweater, Tammy looked older than her thirty seven years. Her dirty blond hair was cut short and the skin on her face looked loose and wrinkled. The Arizona sun and an abusive ex-husband took their toll on her complexion, but not her smile. She stood up and gave Johnny a hug as he approached the table.

"I am so glad you called," Tammy said. "You left Sungod so suddenly we were all pretty worried about you. How is life out in the desert?"

"A little too much excitement for me," Johnny replied. "All I wanted was a nice quiet piece of land to grow old on, but that seems to be a little too much to ask for these days." He told her about the offer Red Ruby Real Estate made on his land and the fire and explosion at the trading post. After they each ordered a cheeseburger basket and he ordered an iced tea, he told her about discovering the Dvoraks on the peak.

"That must have been hard for you," Tammy said. "I know the girl worked at Sungod. Did you know her well?"

"I saw her around at some of the department meetings, but I don't think I ever talked to her," Johnny said. "Did you know her at all?"

"No, but I did go to lunch with the secretary from her program the other day and she was very upset," Tammy said. "She was pretty close to her."

"What did she say about her?" Johnny asked as the food arrived.

Tammy waited for the server to leave and then said, "Just that she was a nice girl. That she was married to some carpenter or someone that didn't bring in much money and that they were moving back to Iowa."

"Did she say why they were moving back?" Johnny asked.

"Her husband got some job at an amusement park and was finally going to make some good money," Tammy said.

"Did she say if Josephine was happy about moving back?" Johnny asked. "Sungod pays pretty well also. It must have been hard to give up all that money."

"You didn't seem to have any trouble giving it up," Tammy said. "Her secretary said that the girl was thinking about having a family. A friend of hers took time off to have a baby and she was a little jealous. It sounded like she might have planned to start a family back there."

"Do you know if there was anyone at work bothering her or if she was having any problems outside of work?" Johnny asked.

Tammy leaned over her plate and whispered, "Her secretary said she came in upset a few weeks ago. A friend of her husband's made a pass at her and she wasn't sure what to do."

"Did she say who the friend was?" Johnny asked.

"I think a tennis partner or something," Tammy said. "It was probably harmless. Her secretary told her to just ignore it and everything would be fine once she got back to Iowa."

"Did she have any prospects for work there?" Johnny asked.

"She was still stuck on the idea of taking some time off to have a baby," Tammy said. "I don't think she told her husband though. I think she wanted to wait to see how the new job worked out before bringing it up."

The two passed the time eating their lunch and exchanging more gossip about people they knew. Johnny felt reassured to hear that nothing had changed since he left the dungeons of Sungod Industries. His old friends were still performing the same mind-numbing tasks and presenting reports of progress to the customer without delivering anything tangible. He paid for the lunch and gave Tammy a goodbye hug before returning to his pickup.

Jim Morrison was starting to look like a possible suspect to Johnny. Knowing that he would be finished with his Sunday morning patrol in time to meet Morrison at his usual Sunday morning tennis match, Johnny dialed Morrison's number on his cell phone.

"I was wondering if you need a tennis partner for Sunday," Johnny said when Morrison answered on the other end of the line.

"Why would you be wondering that?" Morrison asked.

"I know Larry was your partner, so I thought you might need someone to replace him," Johnny said. "I enjoyed the match the other night and thought we could break our tie."

After a pause Morrison agreed to the rematch. Johnny hung up the phone and wondered what he expected to happen at the match. Did he expect Morrison to break down and confess on the court after a sound beating served from Johnny's racket?

CHAPTER 20

Johnny Blue checked in with the dispatcher for the Faithful Security Agency at three o'clock on Friday afternoon. "Checkpoint Alpha all secure," he reported into his radio as he locked the access gate to the canal.

"Glad to have you back on board Detective." Charlie Jones responded through the radio. "See any suspicious vehicles you want to investigate?"

"All secure like I said," Johnny replied.

"All right, all secure," Charlie responded. "How did your week go?"

"Not good," Johnny replied. "If you don't mind, I'd like to keep the banter to a minimum. I just want to make my rounds and go home to get some rest."

"Fine," Charlie said. "Just make sure you keep me posted. I don't want to have to send the sheriff out to check up on you. Everybody is on my back to watch you close tonight."

"Yeah, well who is watching you?" Johnny said.

He drove slowly along the canal searching for any evidence of tampering with the chain link fence and for any animals floating in the water. The afternoon sun was to his back as he drove east. He followed the canal as it turned southeast towards the Red Rock Pumping Plant. The plant used six massive pumps to supply water to the farmers along Park Link Drive and the area surrounding Red Rock. The water was pumped directly into the farmer's irrigation canal system. The same pumps were used to pass water along the CAP canal to users downstream in the Marana and Tucson area whenever they requested water.

The hot afternoon sun beat down on the rectangular cement structure. The structure was built below the level of the canal and Johnny drove downhill towards it. The sun reflected off the six silver metal vertical elevators in front of the rectangular-shaped building. Johnny parked his vehicle on the cement pad next to the massive steel rollup doors. He checked the padlocks on the doors and called in his report. The dispatcher acknowledged the report without comment.

Johnny drove his pickup truck to the exit gate, unlocked the gate, drove his vehicle through the opening and then locked the gate behind him. He drove up the asphalt access ramp to the gravel access road built at the same level as the canal and drove towards the east.

A beige colored one hundred fifty foot tall, thirty foot in diameter metal tower stood alone in the desert two miles away. The tower was used as a buffer to relieve any pressure on the canal caused by surge in water flow. Johnny drove towards the tower along the gravel road. The canal was no longer visible above ground. Six two-mile long underground pipes were used to allow the pumping station to raise the water two hundred fifty feet in elevation before the water began the final leg of its open canal journey to the Tucson area.

Johnny approached the tower, checked the locks on the access gate and then called in his report. He proceeded another mile down the gravel access road to where the discharge pipes resurfaced and dumped their water into the open canal which led to the Marana area. He checked the locks on the access gate and reported the checkpoint all secure. The next stop on his patrol was Picacho Peak State Park.

The peak immediately came in to view as he drove west along the canal. From the ridge along the pumping plant, the peak looked like a sore thumb sticking up in the middle of the desert. He drove slowly down the access road to Park Link Drive, made a left turn, and then turned right on Frontage Road towards the peak. A few minutes later he reached the parking lot outside the park gate and stopped his pickup truck.

He got out of his vehicle, checked the padlock and then surveyed the area. The Dvorak's SUV was no longer parked outside the gift shop. Johnny assumed that the sheriff had the vehicle towed away earlier in the week. He wondered if anyone examined the clothes and the water bottles in the vehicle as possible evidence of a crime. He wondered if a toxicology test had been performed on the bodies or any of the water bottles involved in the incident. He wondered if the vomit Mike Gerrity told him about had been tested or was the incident treated as an open and shut case of accidental death by heat stroke as the sheriff seemed to indicate. That was not his problem, he thought, his problem was to protect the State Park and CAP canal from unwanted intruders.

He looked around for signs of the blue crystals he had found on the previous Sunday evening. No trace was left. He wondered if the police discovered, as he had, that the crystals were a pesticide deadly to woody shrubs such as cotton. He wondered if the sheriff was too focused on finding the killers of the illegal aliens to care.

The smell of charred wood filled his nose as a slow breeze blew in from the east. He got in his pickup and drove to the parking lot of the now destroyed Indian trading post. The giant foam Indian was cut off at the knees by the inferno that knocked Johnny unconscious a few days earlier. A chain link fence guarded the burned out remains of the building.

It looked like the firemen had let the place burn to the ground. That was to be expected for such a remote location. They would have sent out only one tanker and if they ran out of water before the fire was out they would have nothing with which to protect the surrounding area.

Johnny knew from the look of the melted remains of the building that the fire must have been extremely hot. The news report on the radio said that the fire marshal determined that the fire was accidental and caused by an electrical short in the back of the building.

Johnny wondered if anyone bothered to find out why the truck was parked in the empty storage room at the back of a building that had been abandoned for the last two years. He was sure that if the sheriff even bothered to call Red Ruby Real Estate, the registered owner of the building, they would have a satisfactory explanation and no one would pursue the matter any further.

Johnny called the dispatcher and reported Checkpoint Charlie all secure. He got in his pickup and drove away from Marcie's Restaurant headed towards Checkpoint Delta. He had not seen Marcie since the ride home from the hospital. He planned to stop by the restaurant for dinner after his patrol.

Johnny traveled northwest on Frontage Road. He turned onto the dirt road that led to the State Trust Land and abruptly stopped when he noticed a large blue SUV parked on the other side of the closed gate.

CHAPTER 21

Johnny drove through the opening in the fence that led to the State Trust Land. He got out of his pickup to examine the dark blue late model SUV parked alongside the road. He moved to the back of the vehicle and wrote down the license plate number on his small notepad. He noticed several bumper stickers on the back window espousing the views of an environmentalist.

Johnny recognized the vehicle and the stickers as the same ones he saw when he left Marcie's Restaurant to check out the fire at the trading post. Johnny read some of the slogans to himself: "Ban Genetically Engineered Food," "Buy Organic," "Save the Whales," and "No Blood for Oil." The slogans were typical of the environmentalist point of view, Johnny thought. He wondered what the world would be like if this guy got everything he hoped for. Johnny wanted peace and solitude for himself but he was not ready to live like a caveman.

His thoughts were interrupted by a man with a gray beard wearing a white bicycle helmet and riding a yellow mountain bike. Johnny waved at the man as he approached. The man stepped off his bicycle and took off his helmet revealing his long white ponytail. His bright yellow polyester biking suit was drenched in sweat. The man held out his hand for Johnny to shake.

"Hi, I'm John Melnack," he said. "I recognize you from the fire the other day."

"Johnny Blue," Johnny said as he shook the man's hand. "I guess you didn't stick around too long after you reported the fire. The sheriff was asking about you."

"There was nothing I could do," Melnack said. "I figured the fire department would put out the fire and that would be the end of it."

"I think the sheriff would like you to give him a call," Johnny said. "If you wouldn't mind calling his office and asking to speak to Deputy Juan Dugas and tell him I told you to call, I'd appreciate it. He would just like to know what you saw."

"I didn't see much," Melnack said as he loaded his mountain bike on the bike rack on top of his vehicle. "I was just driving by and happened to see the smoke. I pulled into the restaurant because I knew it would have a phone."

"Were you out riding your bike around here that day too?" Johnny asked. "I noticed you did not have it on top of your vehicle when you pulled into the restaurant."

"No, I was coming back from Phoenix on the interstate," Melnack said. "I saw the plumes of smoke and pulled off to warn somebody."

"Do you bike out in this area very much?" Johnny asked.

"A little," Melnack said. "This time of year is a little hot, but when I stopped by the other day I remembered what a fun ride it was out to Wymola Bluff, so I thought I'd come out this afternoon and relive some old memories." He wiped the sweat from his brow.

"I am just on my way to patrol the canal to make sure there isn't anything suspicious going on," Johnny said. "Did you notice anything unusual on your ride?"

"No, just that it was hot out there?" Melnack said as he took a drink of water from a squeeze bottle. "What kind of suspicious activity are you looking for?"

"Did you see any vehicles out there?" Johnny asked. "Was there anyone prowling around? Did you maybe see any blue crystals on the ground out there?"

"I don't know what you are getting at," Melnack said. "But I didn't see anything unusual."

"I heard a story about a guy who looked like you that tried to dump some poison into one of the farmer's irrigation canals in Marana earlier this year," Johnny said. "Was that you?"

"It wasn't poison; it was soap crystals," Melnack said. "I thought that if I could convince the farmer's that there was something wrong with their irrigation water they would not be able to water their bioengineered cotton and might lose their crops. I thought the soap would make the water foam up so they would not take a chance on watering their crops. It was a stupid idea and I got caught before I even poured any into the canal."

"Why did you want to ruin the cotton crops," Johnny asked.

"Because I don't like people playing God with the environment," Melnack said. "The more these farmers try to engineer their crops to keep away the pests, the more Mother Nature is going to fight back by producing super-bugs that will destroy not only the engineered crops, but the organic ones as well."

"So where are we supposed to get the cotton for that T-shirt and those shorts I saw you wearing the other day?" Johnny asked.

"Hey man," Melnack said. "People have been growing cotton for a lot of years without this biotech stuff interfering."

"But aren't all commercially grown crops engineered to a certain extent?" Johnny said. "Our civilization couldn't survive on the kind of corn, wheat and cotton that occurs organically in nature. It has all been engineered through hybridizing over centuries. Do you expect people to walk around naked and gather nuts and berries to survive?"

"You don't get it man," Melnack said. "These people are playing God and they are going to destroy the earth if they aren't stopped."

"I guess you have a point," Johnny said hoping to calm the man down and get back on his good side. "If you do see anything suspicious, I hope you'll notify the sheriff."

Johnny watched the man get in his vehicle and drive through the open gate. Johnny closed the gate behind him, got inside his pickup truck and continued towards Checkpoint Delta.

CHAPTER 22

The sun beat down on his left arm as Johnny drove his pickup along the dirt road towards Checkpoint Delta near the Central Arizona Project canal in the foothills of the Picacho Mountain Range. He noticed that Melnack's bicycle tracks turned down a dirt road towards the southeast in the direction of Wymola Bluff, just as the cyclist had claimed. Johnny reached the checkpoint, unlocked the gate, drove through, locked the gate behind him, surveyed the area and then reported Checkpoint Delta all secure.

He drove slowly along the canal. By the time he reached Checkpoint Echo at the Picacho Pumping Plant, his eyes were weary from looking. He checked the locks on the gates near the pumping plant and called in Checkpoint Echo all secure. He drove to the Brady Pumping Plant, checked the gates and doors and called in Checkpoint Foxtrot all secure. He turned around and drove slowly back the way he came towards Checkpoint Golf, the checkpoint where he had found the pile of blue crystals and the tire tracks.

He wondered how much effort the State Police were putting in on the case. Did Mike Gerrity share his concern about something strange going on out here or did he think Johnny was a paranoid kook? Mike seemed like a stand-up guy. Johnny wondered if he had convinced his superiors to bring in the Homeland Security Department.

He stopped at Checkpoint Golf. The lock on the gate was secure. There were no signs of the blue crystals or the tire tracks. As he suspected, the rains from the monsoon on Monday night had washed them away. Johnny looked at the small mound of lava rock known as Wymola Bluff over a quarter of a mile away from him. It would not provide much cover, he thought. He stared in that direction and realized that he could not see the gas station or restaurant behind the peak.

His imagination was running away with him. It was pretty far fetched to believe that someone picked this particular point to poison the canal just because it was hidden from view from the local establishments.

Johnny watched the traffic pass by on the interstate behind where the restaurant and gas station should be. The bluff certainly would not provide protection from the prying eyes of drivers on the freeway. Maybe that was a chance they were willing to take. Maybe they thought that the chances of a local driving by in the middle of a hot summer day were pretty slim. Who were *they* and what was *their* business, Johnny wondered.

He wondered if John Melnack could be involved at all. Eco-terrorists were as great a danger as foreign terrorists in Johnny's opinion. Melnack had some views that were not well thought out, but he did not seem like a big threat. The story of him dumping soap crystals in the irrigation canal was laughable. On the other hand it gave him an established modus operandi which fit with the blue crystals near the canal. Could he have tried to expand his activities to poison the CAP canal? Johnny found the idea a little hard to believe.

He reported Checkpoint Golf all secure and finished his patrol. He locked the gate to the canal access road adjacent and reported Checkpoint Hotel all secure. "Picacho Patrol signing off," Johnny said into the two-way radio.

"Okay," Charlie, the dispatcher, replied. "I hope we have as much fun doing this again tomorrow."

CHAPTER 23

"Well look who that cat dragged in," Marcie said as Johnny Blue walked into the restaurant. Johnny greeted his friend and ordered his usual cheeseburger with fries and a Diet Coke. He sat down at a booth along the wall and stared through the back window of the restaurant at the saddle-shaped peak outside. The peak threw long shadows towards the east as the evening sun faded in the west.

Marcie sat across the table from Johnny. "We haven't seen you all week," she said. "I hope you have been resting that head of yours. How are you feeling?"

"My head is all better," Johnny said. "It cleared up on Wednesday morning. I felt well enough to put up some straw-bale walls for my house the last two nights."

"That's great," Marcie said. "You'll have to have me over sometime to see it."

"It's not done yet," Johnny said. "I still have to pin the bales together with rebar, get the roof put on and then wrap the outside walls in chicken wire and stucco them. Then I'll have to finish off the interior walls. There is a lot of work still to be done."

"I'm starting to have second thoughts about what I'm doing out there," he said. "I moved out to my ranch for some peace and quiet and look what I've gotent: two dead bodies, a headache from an explosion and Red Ruby pressuring me to sell."

"Red Ruby wants your place, too?" Marcie asked. "I heard he's made some pretty good offers to some of your neighbors out there. I wonder what he is up to."

"I looked at a map and all those small parcels near my property are surrounded by State Trust Land," Johnny said. "I smell another land swap like the one they pulled off in Marana.

"I'm tired of this. I didn't move out here for this stuff, quite the opposite. I guess the desert is no place to hide. For that matter, retirement is no place to hide either."

He heard the ding of the order up bell behind him and Marcie excused herself to retrieve his order from the counter.

"After Carol and Jerry died I saw myself doing some traveling when I retired," Johnny said after Marcie returned with his meal. "Then I bought this property thinking I could settle down and hide from the world. I am starting to think that was wrong. It isn't right to hide from the world. I have a God-given heart and soul and it would be a sin to waste them out here alone."

Marcie smiled and nodded her head as Johnny took a big bite of his burger.

"Have you ever been to Black Canyon of the Gunnison?" Johnny asked.

Marcie shook her head no.

"I took Carol and Jerry there once," he said. "It's a very peaceful place up in Central Colorado. You camp on top of a flat mesa right next to a gorge cut out of solid stone by millions of years of water and wind erosion. I think I should hook up the trailer and drive up there the week after next after I get the walls finished and the roof on my house.

"The drive alone is worth the trip. You climb up passes over eleven thousand feet in elevation and pass through a couple of quaint alpine villages. It really is spectacular."

"That sounds like an excellent idea," Marcie said. "It'll give you time to think. All the stuff that has happened this week, you know that isn't normal. Let things cool off a while and then if you still feel the same way you can take off on the road like you said.

"You probably have enough money saved up to live on the road for a while without selling your place don't you?"

"You know you are right." Johnny said. "All this stuff that is happening, that has nothing to do with me. I could take off and see the country maybe.

"What about you, do you ever take a vacation?'

"You know this place would fall apart without me," Marcie said.

"How about shutting down for a week," Johnny said. "Business is slow. The snowbirds won't be coming down here for a couple of more months. Give Carlos and Shauna a week off with pay to relax and come back happy employees."

Marcie looked over Johnny's shoulder behind the counter where Carlos the cook was flipping through the newspaper for the third time that day.

"You may be right," she said. "I'll have to think about it."

Johnny told her more about his experiences at Black Canyon and the drive through the Rockies in Colorado. Marcie listened intently. At closing time Johnny stood up and walked towards the door.

"I'll be by tomorrow after my shift," he said.

He walked out to his pickup in the fading sunlight.

CHAPTER 24

When he arrived home at his trailer, Johnny saw the rebar laid out inside his newly constructed straw-bale walls and knew that he had a lot of work to do. He took a quick shower in front of his trailer and then changed into short pants and a T-shirt. He set to work pinning the rows of straw-bales together using the metal rods.

The final task in putting up the walls of the house was to pin the bales from the top down using eight foot tall lengths of rebar. The lengths of rebar were already laid out inside the structure.

He donned his work gloves and approached the ladder sitting on the foundation within the confines of the straw-bale walls. He climbed the ladder with a piece of rebar in one hand and a small sledgehammer in the other. He climbed as high as he could above the final row of straw bales, positioned the rebar on top of one of the end bales and drove it down into the bale as far as he could with his hands. Next he stood up above the top end of the rebar and began slowly and methodically pounding the metal rod through the bales until it reached the foundation below. The top of the rebar was barely visible through the upper bale.

He repeated the process until every bale was joined with every bale below it by a solid piece of steel. The work was tedious and dangerous. He was required to climb almost to the top of the twelve foot step-ladder and several times nearly fell as it wobbled with every beat of his hammer on the metal rods he pounded through the bales.

Once he had pinned all the bales and ensured that each was connected to the ones above and below it and locked into place by the rebar, he took a step back to admire his work. The work was exhausting and he was ready to quit for the night. He had only one more task to complete.

The corner of the walls needed to be pinned together using special four foot long U-shaped rebar. He laid out four of the pieces near the corners of the structure. He grabbed one of the bent metal rods and his sledge hammer and then climbed back up the ladder. Johnny positioned the rod such that one leg of the U rested on the bale on one side of a corner and the other leg rested on the top of the other side of the corner. He pounded the bent rod into the two bales until it was barely visible above the straw. He ensured the corner bales were tightly locked together and then repeated the process for the other three corners of the structure.

Johnny sat back down on his plastic chair with a glass of iced tea. It had taken him four hours to complete the pinning. He was exhausted and his clothes were soaked with sweat. It was after twelve o'clock midnight. He felt satisfied. The half moon began to sink behind the Picacho Mountain Range in the distance.

The structure was nearly complete. He would cover it with plastic to keep out the moisture and have the inspector look at it the next week. Then he would have the roofers come in and put on the roof and the plumber and electrician come in and do their work. He would plaster and finish the exterior and interior walls, doors and windows himself. He still had a lot of work to do.

He leaned back in his chair with a feeling of accomplishment. He wondered what the future would be like in his new home.

CHAPTER 25

Johnny Blue awoke to the sound of footsteps outside his trailer. He had gone directly to sleep after covering the newly built straw-bale walls with plastic the night before. He glanced at the clock in his kitchen and saw that the time was four o'clock in the morning. He held his breath and listened to make sure he was not imagining the sound.

The sound of a liquid splashing on the ground made him sit up straight. He jumped out of bed and ran towards his trailer door. He stood listening without breathing for a minute and then swung the trailer door open and peered out into the moonless night. A shadowy figure ran past the trailer towards the driveway.

"Hey," Johnny yelled. "Who's there?" He stepped back inside and grabbed the flashlight off the table in his trailer.

When he returned to the steps outside his door the sandy desert floor reflected the light from flames of a roaring fire near the straw-bale structure he had built. He dropped the flashlight and ran to the makeshift outdoor shower. He ripped the hose from its hook, turned on the water and rushed towards the burning structure. The air smelled of gasoline, melted plastic and burning straw.

He knew that the straw bales would not burn very well on their own, but with a powerful accelerant like gasoline they could send off sparks that might set the surrounding area on fire. He sprayed water on the flames as they climbed up the plastic covering around the straw. He extinguished the fire in a matter of seconds and the dark night surrounded him once again.

Johnny picked up the flashlight where he had dropped it near the trailer steps. Shining the light at the structure, he saw a light smoky steam curling away from the black patches of charred straw where the fire had burned. The black plastic that covered the rest of the straw flapped in the wind. A red gasoline can sat in the sandy soil a few feet away from the structure.

He assumed that he must have startled whoever lit the fire and that they ran off before finishing their work. He wondered who would do something like this. Obviously it was someone trying to send him a message. If they wanted to kill him they would have set the trailer on fire.

He wondered if he should call the sheriff now or wait until the morning light. He did not think he was in any immediate danger and he was sure the culprit was long gone, but delaying the report might look suspicious. He went back into his trailer, turned on the lights inside, picked up his cell phone and dialed the number to the sheriff's office. He explained the situation to the night dispatcher and she indicated that a deputy would be by within the hour.

Johnny sat on a white plastic patio chair bathed in the light from his trailer and waited for the sheriff to arrive. The windmill rudder creaked in the wind as he stared at the metal structure in the middle of the desert. He had unlocked the gate at the end of the driveway to allow the sheriff to drive to the trailer rather than walk. After an hour of staring at the starry sky, Johnny heard the sheriff's vehicle making its way down his driveway.

The light from his trailer was overtaken by the halogen spotlight Deputy Sheriff Juan Dugas aimed at him as his vehicle approached. The deputy was not smiling when he stepped out of his car with a clipboard in his hand.

"What have you got yourself into this time?" he asked.

Johnny shaded his eyes from the spotlight and said, "I've been sitting here thinking about that myself. I pretty much burned all my bridges behind me before I moved out here to get some peace and quiet. That leads me to believe that unless this is some random act of violence it must have something to do with what has occurred since I moved out here.

"I keep to myself except for that security job and up until last Sunday that job was without incident. Since then I've found two dead bodies, watched a trading post burn and explode, spent a few hours in the hospital, witnessed a bunch of illegal aliens wreck out on the interstate, played some tennis with an old partner that knew the dead people, built the walls for my house which are now destroyed, and pretty much rejected an offer to sell this place for twice what I bought it for two months ago. Now you tell me what I've got myself into."

"Rough week, huh?" the Sheriff said as he handed the clipboard to Johnny. "You know the drill by now. Just write down what happened and we'll take a look at it.

"Mind if I look around?"

"I consider this a crime scene so I would be more than happy to have you look around," Johnny said.

He sat back down on the plastic chair and began filling out the witness form. The sheriff turned on a flashlight and aimed it towards the charred straw-bale structure. He scouted the area for a few minutes and then walked back to Johnny.

"That your gas can over there?" the deputy asked.

"Nope," Johnny said. "I think I might have startled whoever started the fire and they dropped it and ran."

"Did you get a look at the culprit?" the deputy asked.

"Just a shadow in the night," Johnny said. "I didn't have any light and by the time I got the flashlight the fire was going."

"You didn't turn on the light inside?" the deputy asked.

"Not at first; I was still groggy and not thinking too clearly," Johnny said.

"All right," the deputy replied. "I'll have the State Police come out to collect evidence and take some pictures. Just leave everything as it is until they get done."

"By the way," he said. "The State Police and Border Patrol pulled over that blue pickup you gave me the license for. Turns out it was an illegal alien smuggler and he had an automatic rifle with him that matches the type used in those two attacks around Red Rock.

"We are waiting on ballistics, but from what one of his partners told the State Police it looks like this is the guy responsible. I guess he could not handle all the people waiting at the pick-up location so he decided to thin them out a little by shooting them and taking their money.

"That was quick thinking to get the license plate like that. You are a hero."

Johnny blushed and smiled at the deputy as he handed him the witness report. He was not sure if the deputy was sincere or making some kind of sarcastic reference to the Richard Jewell character he had mentioned to Mike Gerrity.

"What about those militia guys you handcuffed," Johnny asked. "I thought maybe they were the ones doing the attacks on the illegals with all those guns they had."

"We charged them with a couple of misdemeanor reckless endangerments and false imprisonments and then put them on probation," the sheriff said. "As part of their probation they have to go back to California where they came from and stay away from any militia activities in Arizona. They are California's problem now."

The deputy took the report from Johnny and then drove away in his car. Johnny went back inside his trailer and laid down on his bed as the dark blue sky changed to light blue with the rising of the sun.

CHAPTER 26

Johnny heard the sound of a vehicle pulling up next to his trailer. He got off his bed and looked outside to see Officer Mike Gerrity getting out of his white Crown Victoria Department of Public Safety vehicle. The digital clock in the kitchen read 9:00 A.M. Johnny stretched his arms over his head, yawned, and walked outside to greet the officer.

"So you just can't stay out of trouble can you Johnny," the officer said with a smile. He surveyed the charred bales of hay and red gas can nearby and then turned back to Johnny. "Any idea who did this?"

"Like I told the sheriff," Johnny said. "My life had been pretty quiet until I found those two bodies last week. I can't see how this could be related to that. I am not a criminal or violent person, so it would be hard for me to put myself in the shoes of whoever started the fire and understand why they did it."

"Let's go over everything else has happened to you this week," the officer said.

"After finding the bodies on the peak there was the explosion at the trading post. You know about that," Johnny said. "Then I started checking into those crystals with a guy I knew at Sungod. Turns out they are some kind of herbicide."

"We just got the results back from the lab yesterday and found the same thing," the officer said. "In fact we found out that a large quantity of that herbicide was reported missing by a certain developer in the area. We are still checking into it. What else?"

"This guy I used to play tennis with emailed me and wanted me to play," Johnny said. "It turns out he used to play with Larry Dvorak, the dead guy I found on the peak. We played and I started to suspect that he might have something to do with the deaths."

"What made you suspect that?" the officer asked.

"I found out that diuretics can cause dehydration pretty quickly," Johnny said. "I have a hunch he is using diuretics as a way to lose water weight so he looks better when he goes out in public. I know it's crazy. But he also was late for his tennis match the morning the Dvoraks went on their hike and I heard a rumor that he had some trouble with Josephine Dvorak."

"An interesting theory," the officer said as he made notes on a small pad. "But it's all pretty circumstantial. Does he know you suspect him?"

"I am not sure," Johnny said. "I mentioned a few things about the deaths and he seemed to get a little irritated."

"Did anything else happen to you this week?" the officer asked.

"Red Ruby Real Estate made me an offer on my place for twice what I paid for it," Johnny said. "I gave them every indication that I wasn't interested. I know Ruby has a reputation for playing hardball, but would he go this far to scare me off?"

As he spoke, a team of officers, some in uniform and some wearing plain clothes with an official jacket identifying them as investigators for the Homeland Security Department, walked towards Johnny and Officer Gerrity.

"Excuse me a minute," Officer Gerrity said to Johnny. The officer greeted the investigators, gave them directions and then returned to Johnny.

"These guys are going to gather up the evidence here, but I am pretty sure I know what they'll find," the officer said. "Let me clue you in a little so you don't have to worry. The herbicide you found is pretty dangerous. It is so deadly that it has to be registered with the federal government. An audit of the inventory of a certain real estate developer found a large quantity of the herbicide unaccounted for a few weeks ago. I can't tell you which developer, but we have been keeping tabs on him since the discrepancy showed up in the audit."

"So you think it was a developer trying to scare the farmers off their land, not some eco-terrorist?" Johnny said. "I heard about a white haired man with a ponytail trying to poison the irrigation canals earlier in the year. And then last night I ran into him out by the CAP canal."

"I know who you are talking about," the officer said. "I investigated that case. It was soap crystals he was trying to dump in the irrigation canal.

"He is strictly small-time. He wouldn't be involved in anything like what we have going on here. He called the sheriff last night about the trading post fire. The sheriff had him call me and I believe his story.

"From what he said, I figured it was you that told him to call in. That was good thinking."

"I don't know what to think anymore," Johnny said. "There is too much going on. I hope you have a handle on it all."

"We have been investigating the developer and the missing herbicide as a possible prelude to a terror attack," the officer said. "That has allowed us to set up some strategic wiretaps to get more information.

"As you can see I took your advice and brought in the Homeland Security Department to help us out. From everything you have told me and with the information from the wiretaps, I am pretty sure who is responsible for this.

"We were planning to take them into custody as soon as we got a little more concrete evidence. I think we can connect this incident to some of the others and take them into custody tonight. You don't have to worry about them coming back. You are a hero Johnny."

Johnny frowned and shook his head. He knew Mike Gerrity well enough to know that he was sincere in what he said. Even if he did allow himself to believe what was said about him, which he would not, it contradicted his plan to lead a simple quiet life in the desert. He tried to get himself to think in the present and not imagine the label as something that would stick with him the rest of his life.

Johnny excused himself and went back inside his trailer. He sat down in front of his laptop, plugged his headphones into the back of the computer, and began playing his meditation tape.

He closed his eyes and listened to Carol's voice invade his thoughts. A blurry vision of his wife's face appeared in his mind. He stared at the face and listened as it spoke words of encouragement to him. Suddenly the skin began to melt away from the vision to reveal a clean white human skull. Red skin slowly reformed itself on the white bone structure until Josephine Dvorak's parched face formed in his mind.

CHAPTER 27

By eight o'clock Saturday night the investigative crews had collected their evidence and Johnny had completed the Saturday morning and Saturday evening patrols without incident. He sat at his usual booth eating his usual meal talking with Marcie. Johnny told her about the fire at his house and the subsequent investigation.

"I've decided that tomorrow is going to be my last patrol for the Faithful Security Agency," Johnny said.

"Oh really," Marcie said. "You made the decision that quick?"

"I only took the job because it was convenient and I thought it would be simply be a matter of checking to make sure all the gates were locked," Johnny said. "I guess nothing is easy. You can't expect to take a job like that and not have to face the wrong element. Society expects someone to protect them from that element and I don't think I'm the type to do it.

"I'm more of the starving artist type. Maybe I'll take up painting."

"You've got to follow your heart," Marcie said. "What's it telling you now?"

"It's telling me that I've got to keep searching for a meaningful way to contribute to society," Johnny said. "I served my country in the Navy when I was young, but my heart was not in it. There's nothing wrong with self-sacrifice, but like you said, you have to follow your heart.

"I spent four years in college learning to be an engineer and applied my skills at Sungod helping to build devices to protect this country. Again my heart was not in it. That kind of work came easy to me and I never once challenged myself.

"I tried making a family and that was destroyed in an instant. I tried protecting this community from terrorists and other bad guys and have failed at that.

"My heart says to stop trying to fill the shoes of society's concept of a strong protective man and try to bring joy into someone's life instead. My heart says I need to spend some time at Black Canyon of the Gunnison thinking about my future."

"Does your heart say whether or not you want any company?" Marcie asked as she rested her right hand on top of his left hand in the middle of the table.

"Yes it does," Johnny said. "We can leave Monday if you are ready. I have everything we need. You just need to bring some clothes and your smile."

"What about your house," Marcie said. "Don't you want to finish that before the next monsoon rains arrive?"

"Yeah, I guess you are right," Johnny said. "The damage to the bales weren't as bad as I first thought. I'll have to replace a small section, but I have enough extra bales to do that."

"I'll tell you what," Johnny said. "Let's make it Wednesday. That way I'll have time to fix the walls, get them inspected, cover them in plastic and get the roofer out there to put on the roof while I'm gone. Everything is falling into place. I just hope nothing happens to mess it up."

"Pick me up at my place on Wednesday morning," Marcie said.

"How does ten o'clock sound," Johnny said.

"I can't wait," Marcie replied.

Johnny whistled a melody with no particular tune as he walked outside into the fading sunlight. The air was warm. It felt like just the right temperature. He reminded himself to call his boss first thing in the morning. He wanted to let Mike Gerrity and Deputy Dugas know he was leaving town also.

He remembered that he still had a tennis date with Jim Morrison between patrols the next day. No need to cancel that, he thought. Originally he had planned to confront Morrison about his dealings with the Dvoraks, but now he thought he would just let it go. He was through with the security guard business and through playing the role of an amateur sleuth. Let the professionals handle it, he thought.

As he parked his pickup truck next to his travel trailer home, his cell phone rang.

"You don't know me," a male voice whispered through the phone when Johnny answered it. "But I believe you found my daughter on Picacho Peak."

CHAPTER 28

Johnny talked with the father of Josephine Dvorak for over an hour before hanging up. He felt sorry for the man. The stated reason for the call was to thank Johnny for finding his daughter, but Johnny felt that there was more going on.

It was clear that the man loved his daughter very much. He had asked for Johnny's opinion on whether her death was an accident or if something else could have happened. Johnny gave him the politically correct answer that he was sure the authorities could say better than he and that by all accounts it appeared to be an accident.

"We just received a letter she mailed before she died," the father had said. "She was very excited about moving back to Iowa near us and maybe starting a family of her own. She mentioned that one of Larry's friend's was creeping her out, as she put it. She was ready to come home and restore her old friendships."

"Did she identify who the friend was?" Johnny asked.

"Just some tennis playing buddy of Larry's," the father replied. "Why? Do you know who it could be?"

"No, just curious," Johnny said. He felt it was better to let sleeping dogs lie. It was better to let him think the best and if it turned out that it really was an accident they could all sleep better.

If Morrison was involved in Josephine's death in any way Johnny would be contributing to society by exposing him for what he was. Josephine's father would appreciate knowing the truth and the world would be a better place. He sat down on his plastic patio chair and sipped on his iced tea. He had tennis on his mind.

He realized that he was not a detective and he needed help. Deputy Sheriff Dugas seemed less than eager to take him seriously. He thought of Mike Gerrity, the State Police Officer that had helped him when his wife died. He picked up his cell phone and dialed the number for the officer's home.

After exchanging preliminary greetings, Johnny got right down to the case. He explained the circumstantial evidence against Morrison including the possible use of diuretics as part of a dangerous diet plan, his relationship with the deceased husband and the rumors of harassment of the deceased wife. The officer responded with information that the toxicology report had just came back positive for a high amount of a diuretic in the blood stream and that one of the empty water bottles found in the couple's backpack contained trace amounts of the substance.

"What about the blood spots on their hands and legs?" Johnny asked.

"They turned out to be the result of an encounter with a cholla," the officer replied.

"I made a date to play tennis with the guy tomorrow between my patrols," Johnny said. "Originally I thought I might confront him, then I decided to let you professionals handle it. After talking with Josephine's father, I want to nail this guy. What can I do?"

CHAPTER 29

Johnny Blue walked slowly towards the entrance of the Marana Tennis Club. His normally loose tennis shorts felt unusually uncomfortable and he knew why. He noticed Jim Morrison's black sports car parked near the entrance to the building, so he knew Morrison would be waiting for him. What he did not know was whether or not Jim Morrison suspected that there was more to the morning's meeting than just a game of tennis. Johnny signed in with the young Hispanic woman busy with her school homework behind the receptionist counter.

Johnny walked slowly towards the outside tennis courts. The day was already warm. The bright sun beat down on his forehead as he walked outside.

"It's not too hot to play is it?" Johnny quipped as he approached the court on which Morrison was practicing his serve.

"I'm game if you are," Morrison replied. He walked over to Johnny, smiled and held out his hand. Johnny shook Morrison's hand and then wiped his own hand on his shorts.

"Have to break that tie," Johnny replied. "I think we both won one set last Wednesday."

"Let's play," Morrison said.

"Let's," Johnny said as he walked out onto the court. "How about a break after every three games? It's kind of hot and I don't want to get dehydrated."

Morrison agreed and the players took their positions with Morrison serving first. He held his serve and the players switched sides. Johnny held his serve also. Morrison had trouble holding his serve from the court facing southeast into the morning sun. After several scores of Deuce and Advantage, Morrison subdued Johnny and the score was Morrison two games and Johnny one.

They met at the bench between courts and each drank heavily from their squeeze bottles.

"So you and Larry used to play on Sundays, huh," Johnny said.

"Yeah we played Wednesdays and Sundays just like you and I used to," Morrison said.

"I guess I'm not as irreplaceable as I think," Johnny said and took another drink of water. "Did you ever meet his wife?"

"I think you asked me that last Wednesday," Morrison said. "I said I may have seen her one time maybe. Are you ready to play?"

"Looks like I'm out of water," Johnny said. "Let me go fill up my bottle and I'll be right back."

"Wait I have an extra one right here," Morrison said as he dug through his bag. "This one is especially for you."

Johnny took a drink from the bottle of water and noticed a slightly odd taste. "This water is the same brand the Dvoraks were drinking that morning they died," he said.

Morrison let the comment pass.

The two resumed their positions on the court with Johnny now serving into the sun. He held his serve after surviving a few scores of Deuce. Morrison easily held his serve and the two opponents switched sides. Johnny held his serve from the side facing away from the sun. The two men returned to the bench between

the courts. All other courts were empty in the hot sun.
The score was tied at three games apiece.

"It must be a hundred and seven degrees out
here," Johnny said as he drank from the bottle. "Tell me
Jim, why did you only ask me to play on Wednesday.
Didn't you need a replacement for Larry last Sunday?"

"He canceled on Saturday," Morrison said. "He
said he was going hiking instead. I thought it was too
short of notice, so I didn't call you."

"So you didn't play last Sunday?" Johnny said as
he finished the bottle of water.

"No, I checked out a serving machine and just
practiced by myself," Morrison said. "Ready?"

"I'm out again and have to use the restroom. Let
me run in and fill-up and empty, so to speak," Johnny
said.

Johnny walked briskly back to the clubhouse. He
used the restroom and then came back out into the
lobby to fill up his bottle with water from the drinking
fountain. Through the glass windows on the front of the
building, Johnny noticed a light blue Crown Victoria
parked behind Morrison's car. He replaced the cap on
his bottle and walked back out into the sunshine on the
courts.

"You didn't put anything in my water did you,"
Johnny said with a laugh. "All of a sudden my bladder
is filling up faster than I can empty it."

Morrison did not reply.

Morrison held his serve from the side facing the
sun and the two players switched sides. The game went
to Deuce twice before Johnny held his serve. Morrison
held his serve on the next game. The score was
Morrison five games, Johnny four games. The two
retired to the bench for refills of water.

Johnny wiped the sweat from his brow and gulped water from his bottle. "I wonder what it was like for those two up on that peak in the hot sun dying of thirst," Johnny said.

"I have no idea," Morrison said softly. He hung his head and scraped his shoes against the concrete surface.

"I heard that they puked their guts out about halfway down," Johnny said. "It just seems odd that anyone could die that fast even in that kind of heat. It must have taken them only a couple of hours to get to the top and then a half hour later they were puking their guts out. I heard heat exhaustion will do that to you, but it just seems odd that it would set in that fast."

"So what are you saying?" Morrison said.

"I am not saying anything," Johnny said. "I just wanted to get your opinion."

"I have no opinion," Morrison said.

"Even about Josephine?" Johnny asked. "I heard you had a thing for her. I heard you made a pass at her."

"Where'd you hear that?" Morrison asked.

"It's a small town," Johnny said. "I hear things."

"Hey, I stopped by their house one time to see if Larry wanted to play," Morrison said. "He wasn't home and she started to come on to me. We did a little making out and then I told her I couldn't do that to Larry. She must have started spreading rumors saying it was me just to cover her ass. Can we play?"

"Knowing you it must have been hard to turn that down," Johnny said. "I've got to piss and fill up my bottle again."

He ran awkwardly into the building, used the restroom and refilled his bottle with water from the drinking fountain in the lobby. The blue car was still parked behind Morrison's vehicle. Johnny knew what he had to do.

"Ready to finish this off?" Johnny asked as he took his position serving into the sun.

He held his serve easily to tie the set at five games apiece. He showed renewed energy on the court covering everything Morrison hit over the net. The two opponents switched sides and Morrison took his place behind the baseline to serve into the sun.

The game went to Deuce and then Johnny gained the advantage. Morrison served a powerful serve that Johnny barely got his racket on. The ball lifted high in the air over the net. Morrison lifted his left hand over his head to guide his racket as he prepared to smash the ball. He swung the racket down as hard as he could.

Johnny heard a loud swooshing sound as the racket passed by the ball. He watched the ball bounce into Morrison's side of the court and then raised his hands over his head in victory. He had broken Morrison's serve.

"Don't get too excited," Morrison said. "You still have to win by two games."

"I know," Johnny replied. "I'm just happy to break the master's serve."

The score was six games to five and Johnny only needed to hold his serve to win the set and match. The two opponent's switched sides and Johnny prepared to serve facing into the sun.

The game went to Deuce and then Johnny took the advantage. His bladder felt as if it were about to explode as he threw the yellow tennis ball high up over his head. He swung down on the ball and heard a shrill whizzing sound as the ball flew across the court and over the net. The ball landed in the service box on Jim

Morrison's side of the court and jumped up in the air. Morrison swung at the ball but it whizzed by his racket and slammed into the chain link fence. The ball stuck in the fence about three feet above the ground.

Johnny raised his hands in victory, threw his racket high into the air and caught it in his arms as it came down. Morrison slammed his racket into the concrete.

Johnny ran towards the net and jumped over it. He felt the weight shift in his shorts as he landed on Jim Morrison's side of the court. Morrison was down on his knees holding his head in his hands.

"Good game," Johnny said holding out his hand for Morrison. Morrison stood up and gripped Johnny's hand. Johnny pulled him in close and said, "I know you did it Jim. Why don't you tell me how?"

"What are you talking about," Morrison said as he tried to pull away.

Johnny held him close and said, "You went after her didn't you? She rejected you and you thought you'd teach her a lesson didn't you? You didn't want to kill her? You just wanted her to get a little dehydrated so you could hurt her like she hurt you?"

Morrison broke away from Johnny's grip and walked towards his tennis bag near the bench. "You aren't even close," Morrison said as he sat down on the bench with his back to the clubhouse. "All right I'll tell you just because you can't prove anything. That bitch wanted me. I could see it in her eyes, but she claimed that she still loved Larry.

"So I met them before they left for the peak. I brought two bottles of water, one with Lasix and one without. I made sure I gave the doctored one to Larry and the clean one to Josephine. Somehow they must have both drank from the doctored one. I figured it would incapacitate him and she'd come running to me for comfort. She wanted me."

"Jim Morrison," the deep voice of Mike Gerrity came from behind Morrison on the bench. "You are under arrest for the murder of Larry and Josephine Dvorak. Stand up please."

As the officer handcuffed Morrison Johnny pulled the electronic wires and transmitter from out of his shorts. "You didn't think I had that big of a package did you Jim?" he said.

CHAPTER 30

Johnny drove towards Park Link Drive to start his patrol on Sunday afternoon. He thought about the scene at the tennis club. Morrison broke into sobs once the cuffs were on and Officer Gerrity began to read him his rights. Johnny had turned the electronic gear over to Officer Gerrity and then changed into his security guard uniform in the locker room. He felt good that the mystery was solved but his thoughts were dominated by the feeling of regret over the loss of two lives because of the petty ego of a shallow man.

When he signed up to be a security guard he did not take it seriously. He saw himself checking gates and deterring crime by his mere presence. He never thought about the seedier side of the occupation; the side that exposed him to criminals, violence and even death.

He considered what his obligation to society was as a trade for the benefits he received; the benefits of living in seclusion, of eating what he wanted when he wanted, of building his own house out of the materials he wanted to use, and of traveling where he wanted when he wanted. He listened to his thoughts and realized that he sounded like a four year old that could only see his own immediate needs and demanded immediate satisfaction.

Johnny thought about what Marcie said about following his heart. Since his wife and child had died five years earlier he felt as if his heart had died too. He tried to remember what his dreams for the future were like before the accident. He did not mind the drudgery of the work at Sungod at the time. His heart was not in it, but the money and ample time off allowed him to put his energy into his family. At work he thought of Jerry and Carol and was excited to get home to hear about their day. He thought about Carol and the way they worked so well together; the way they knew each others thoughts before they were even spoken.

His heart felt empty. To try to fill it up with some kind of trivial occupation that contributed to society seemed futile. He felt old; too old to start a family anew. He wondered if a relationship was the answer. Could Marcie or anyone else rekindle that flame he lost so many years ago? Could they develop that special relationship where they knew each other's thoughts before they were spoken? If so, then what: settle down and run the restaurant together? Travel from campground to campground in his trailer?

In any case he was starting to have second thoughts about retiring to the desert. The desert, as it turned out, was no place to hide. There was never enough ground cover and resources were so scarce everybody wanted to get their hands on what everyone else already had in their possession. Retirement is no place to hide either. He had lived a good life when he worked as an engineer, but now he had to start thinking like he had been reborn into a new life. Maybe he had just stepped into the light from the birth canal and now he needed to learn and grow as a newly born retired person.

He thought about the Dvoraks. Tammy, the secretary at Sungod, had said that she thought Josephine wanted to have a child. Johnny wondered what would have happened had the couple had a child. Could all of this have been avoided or would there be another orphan in the world? He thought about orphans, maybe he could make a difference with them. He missed Jerry. He wondered how many Jerry's there were in the world with no parents because of people like Jim Morrison. He felt a warm spot growing in his chest.

It would be something to think about on the trip to Black Canyon of the Gunnison.

He listened to the radio on the drive up Interstate 10. A news report said that State Police Officers had arrested Bob O'Rielly and charged him with arranging the arson of the Indian trading post and poisoning the irrigation water for the cotton fields near Red Rock with an herbicide. He was also suspected in arranging another arson and more charges would be filed later. Red Ruby had no comment on the arrest of one of his top employees.

The report said that the public was in no danger from the attempted poisoning of the Central Arizona Project canal. The quantity of herbicide put in the canal was so small that it would have no effect on anyone drinking the water. The water would be treated and any traces of the chemical removed before it was delivered to any drinking water supply.

The herbicide never made it from the CAP canal to the farmer's irrigation canals. CAP's water quality monitoring had detected the presence of the herbicide before it was released into the system. When O'Rielly realized poisoning the CAP supply was not working he changed his plans. He tried adding the poison directly into a farmer's irrigation canal when the monsoon rains hit on Monday. Only a few acres of cotton were ruined. The heat from the investigation of the missing herbicide and the deaths on Picacho Peak caused O'Rielly to order his hired goons to destroy evidence by burning the truck used in delivering the herbicide and the Indian trading post used to hide the truck.

All the loose ends had been tied together. The deaths of the couple had been the work of an egotistical misguided psychopath. The blue crystals and arson fires were an attempt by a greedy land developer to drive farmers and Johnny into selling their land. The murders of the illegal aliens were committed by ruthless smugglers. The militia men had been kicked out of the state for illegally shooting at and holding border crossers against their will.

At eight P.M. Johnny called in to his dispatcher. "Checkpoint Hotel all secure," he said. He looked up at the mystical Picacho Peak as the sun sank low on the horizon. He wondered what stories the mountain could tell if it could talk.

"I'll turn in my radio and uniforms on my way out of town," he said. "Picacho Patrol signing off."

The Johnny Blue Mystery Series

Follow the adventures of Johnny Blue as he travels America's campgrounds solving mysteries and living the dream.

Picacho Peak Mystery

Johnny Blue investigates the mysterious deaths of a young couple in Picacho Peak State Park and suspicious blue crystals near an aqueduct in southern Arizona.

COMING SOON!

Black Canyon Mystery

Johnny Blue and his close friend Marcie solve the mystery behind a lost boy in Black Canyon of the Gunnison National Park in Colorado.

Melting Glaciers Mystery

Johnny and Marcie put themselves in harm's way to solve the mystery behind multiple deaths by drowning in Glacier National Park in Montana.

Orders and Information

www.livingthedreampublishing.com

Living the Dream Publishing
PMB 173
8340 N Thornydale #110
Tucson, Arizona 85741